"What now?"
His eyes were heavy-lidded, his voice the lowest whisper.

Her face was hot, her breasts heavy. Between her legs, she felt the slick wetness of her body's response to him, the insistent clench of inner muscles.

It was inevitable, then. This. Them. Tonight. Now.

"You could kiss me," she said.

For the first time in what seemed like hours, he looked away from her face, to her bare shoulder, which was pressed up near her jawline. Taking all the time in the world, he pulled his hand out of his pocket and slid his long, warm fingers up her arm, to the point that held his absolute attention.

Then he circled with his thumb, leaned in and pressed a kiss to her shoulder. A long, wet, scorching kiss that nearly left her trembling.

His other hand came out of his pocket, and everything happened at once. His hungry, searching mouth ran back and forth over that sweet tendon and continued on its way up her exposed throat, across her cheek, to his final destination—her lips.

Books by Ann Christopher

Kimani Romance

Just About Sex
Sweeter Than Revenge
Tender Secrets
Road to Seduction
Campaign for Seduction
Redemption's Kiss
Seduced on the Red Carpet
Redemption's Touch

ANN CHRISTOPHER

is a full-time chauffeur for her two overscheduled children. She is also a wife, former lawyer and decent cook. In between trips to various sporting practices and games, Target and the grocery store, she likes to write the occasional romance novel. She lives in Cincinnati and spends her time with her family, which includes two spoiled rescue cats, Sadie and Savannah, and a rescue hound, Sheldon. Her next book for Harlequin/Kimani Romance is *The Surgeon's Secret Baby,* a part of the Hopewell General Hospital continuity miniseries, which will be released in September 2011.

If you'd like to recommend a great book, share a recipe for homemade cake of any kind, or suggest a tip for getting your children to do what you say the first time you say it, Ann would love to hear from you through her website, www.AnnChristopher.com.

Redemption's TOUCH

ANN CHRISTOPHER

To Richard

Recycling programs for this product may not exist in your area.

ISBN-13: 978-0-373-86213-9

REDEMPTION'S TOUCH

www.kimanipress.com

Printed in U.S.A.

Dear Reader,

Dawson Reynolds's troubled relationship with the Warner family, which goes back many years, includes secrets, betrayal, bitterness and anger. His plan in returning to Heather Hill is to confront those who have wronged him, demand justice and leave.

He comes armed for battle…ready to fight… determined to win.

The last thing he expects is to meet his match in the form of a Warner niece.

The beautiful and disarming Arianna Smith brings sweetness and light into Dawson's dark and lonely world, and the two of them fall—almost instantly—into each other's arms.

This, of course, complicates Dawson's whole retribution/revenge scheme. Quite a bit. Because it's hard to be mad at the world when you're falling in love with an angel….

Happy reading!

Ann

Acknowledgments

Special thanks to Regina Riggins, R.N.,
for answering my medical questions.
Love you, girl! And to Kelli Martin and Alex Colon at
Kimani Romance, for being so much fun to work with.

Chapter 1

Ten years since I've been here, Dawson Reynolds thought, *and I've done all the changing.* Heather Hill was exactly as he remembered.

Every red brick of the grand old estate seemed familiar, every oak, rose bush and blade of grass on the manicured grounds the same as if he'd seen them yesterday. Heather Hill was almost like an old friend, or a childhood home, except that he wasn't foolish enough to think that he had either friends or a home. No. He had nothing other than his ambition and his agenda, both of which required him to finally return.

So he did.

Tonight was another of Arnetta Warner's glittering fundraisers for Alzheimer's research, the perfect cover for his little reconnaissance mission, and he'd finagled an invitation. Which hadn't been hard once the Warner matriarch heard that he had deep pockets courtesy of his real estate fortune.

Too bad the old girl didn't know that Dawson Reynolds wasn't his birth name. She'd've been a smidge less gracious with the warm welcome if she knew who he really was. But she'd find out soon enough.

Not tonight, though.

Tonight was about getting the lay of the land without being spotted, and he'd learned everything he needed to know.

Was the estate still as over-the-top-opulent as it'd ever been, camera-ready in case some network decided to shoot a new series melodrama like, say, *Dynasty—The Next Generation?*

Check.

Did the diamonds, champagne, cars and designer clothes still abound here, like trash talk during a pickup game of hoops?

Check.

Was Arnetta Warner, the grande dame herself, still shadowed by Franklin Bishop, her sidekick of forty years?

Oh, yeah. That was a big fat check.

Neither of them had spied Dawson; he'd seen to that. In a crowd of several hundred people spread throughout living rooms, music rooms, dining rooms and atriums, spilling out onto terraces and into tents and gazebos, it was easy to cling to the candlelit shadows and blend in.

To watch. To wait. To learn.

He'd discovered that Mrs. Warner, though still beautiful, was entirely white-haired now, her shoulders curved with her eighty-plus years. Franklin Bishop's dark eyes were still sharp, but they looked weary. They'd both slowed down in the last ten years and moved through the crowd with the careful steps of someone afraid of a slip-and-fall.

The bottom line was that they were old.

He'd known it, yeah, but seeing it was a shock.

Get over it, man, he told himself.

Having accomplished everything he came for, it was time to split before someone he knew scoped him out. The real fun started tomorrow.

But…

He'd've liked to hang out here and enjoy the spectacular view. He'd roamed to the far end of one of the many terraces and walkways, the one nearest the greenhouse, and it would've been nice to linger for a minute, listening to the faint notes of jazz coming from the house. The summer night was balmy, the moon high and bright, and his plans were coming together so well he wanted to enjoy life.

More than that, he wanted to meet the woman he'd glimpsed across the dance floor tonight, the beautiful distraction in the electric-blue dress, the one who'd smiled at him and made need contract in his gut. The one who—

No. He wouldn't go there. The last thing he needed was a distraction.

Knocking back the last of his red wine, he set the goblet on the stone ledge, reached inside his jacket for his cell phone and thumbed in the number he'd been given earlier. The valet could bring the car around to meet him in front—

The unexpected click of high heels on the stones behind him was his only warning. That, and the negligible but mind-numbing swish of silk against gleaming skin. And then she was there, the distraction, the woman who'd snagged his unwilling attention and hadn't yet let it go.

He looked over his shoulder at her and froze, the dialed cell phone hovering near his ear and all his best-laid plans going up in smoke.

"Were you ever going to say hi to me?" she asked.

He stared, surprised on so many levels it seemed unlikely he'd ever get his jaw up off the ground. "Hello?" the valet said in his ear, but Dawson hit End and hung up on him, all his focus irrevocably centered on this female.

There was no coyness about her, no false shyness or calculated hesitation, all of which bored him worse than watching white paint dry. She radiated an open curiosity, as though she honestly needed to solve the mystery of why he hadn't approached her when they'd caught each other's eye earlier. As though understanding him mattered to her, a lot.

She was a tiny little thing, young, but everything about her was pure, one-hundred percent, grade-A woman with a capital *W*. Her generous curves—yes, there was a God—were poured into that blue dress, which was slinky like a nightgown and yet not particularly revealing. Her bare arms were toned, her pale brown skin an invitation his twitchy fingers could barely resist. She had a tumble of black curls around her shoulders and a dimple in her chin.

And her eyes.

Jesus. She had the dewy, wide-eyed innocence of a Disney princess, so much so that he felt like the hulking and clumsy Big Bad Wolf next to her.

Only, no Disney princess had ever exuded sex like *this*.

Her mouth curled with open amusement, as though she knew exactly how she made his blood simmer with lust. "Should I repeat the question?"

Finally, several beats too late, his wits reappeared and scrambled to catch up. “No. I wasn’t going to say hi to you.”

She frowned and nodded. “That’s what I thought. So it’s a good thing I took matters into my own hands, isn’t it?”

“Remains to be seen.”

She laughed and it was, like everything else about her, unassuming, sexy and startling. Her voice was high and sweet, but her laugh was deep and throaty, as earthy as sex with the windows open on a rainy night.

That need strengthened, twisting in his gut.

“Here.” She passed him one of the delicate glass bowls she’d been holding and kept one for herself. “Have some dessert with me.”

Saying no wasn’t an option. You didn’t say no when the president tapped you for his cabinet, or when Don Corleone asked for a favor, or when this little walking wet dream wanted to spend time with you. He took it. When the tips of their fingers brushed, he felt a flare of heat spread up his arm and out through the pores of his skin, enough to make him sweat.

The sudden hitch of her breath told him she’d felt it, too, that unholy spark, but she got over it and went back to taking charge. “Sit with me.”

She tried to ease her hip onto the ledge and get comfortable. But she was short, and the wall was high, and he hated to think of her scratching her fine skin or snagging her dress.

That, and he really, really wanted to touch her again.

“Wait.” Without thought, he put his bowl down, planted his hands on the curve of her hips and lifted her to a seated position.

Bad move, Dawson.

She felt so good, so unspeakably *right,* that he almost choked on the sensation. The silk slithered over her hot skin, making him desperate to touch the flesh underneath, and he didn't—physically could not—let her go.

As if that wasn't a challenging enough test of his self-control, something worse happened. From the corner of his eye he saw the bottom of her dress slide away, revealing way more leg than a woman this petite should have, and thighs that he would have killed to sink his teeth into.

All the while, she stared straight into his face with those bright eyes, studying him with unabashed curiosity, and he tried not to feel her breathless stillness between his hands.

Have mercy.

Feeling scalded, he let her go, picked up his bowl again and eased onto the ledge beside her, not touching, but much closer than he should have been. This seemed to make her happy, because she smiled that glorious smile and dug into the dessert.

To give himself something to do until she made her next move, he tasted his, too. It was something chocolate and fluffy—mousse, probably.

"So," she said, enjoying her mousse with a delighted wriggle that made him wonder, with a fierce curiosity, what reactions she had when she had an orgasm, "why didn't you want to speak to me?"

"Didn't seem like a good idea." Sparing her a dark glance, he decided to concentrate on eating. "Still doesn't."

She laughed, taking no offense. "Because I'm younger than you?"

Huh. Younger. His thirty-five suddenly felt like a 150 to her twentyish. "I try to wait until a female's graduated before I approach her, yeah."

Her grin widened. "I'll have you know I just graduated."

"Junior high?"

"Yale Law. Stanford undergrad, in case you're interested."

Figured. She might be young, but there was no dummy lurking behind those sharp eyes. "Congratulations. So what are you doing with yourself now? Besides studying for the bar and approaching strange men at parties?"

"Relaxing. I need a little time off."

There was a story there. Shadows didn't darken faces for no reason, and some compulsion made him ask, "Rough year?"

She hesitated. "You have no idea."

"Try me."

Her gaze dropped to her bowl and stayed there as a flush crept up her neck and over her cheeks. "Well," she began, "among other things, my brother Antonios was killed in Afghanistan."

"Oh, no."

"And his twin, Alessandro—"

Hold up. *"Alessandro?"*

"It's Greek for 'defending men.'"

"Right."

"He was just discharged from the Marines. He was injured in the same attack. He's having a tough time."

"I'm sorry," he said, and he was. But a nagging little twinge of something told him that there was more to her story. Had a man created those shadows in her eyes? And why did that possibility make him want to smash something? "That all? My Spidey-Sense is telling me you had a…bad breakup or something."

"You could say that," she admitted.

But her gaze stayed on that bowl and she clammed up like her tongue had been glued to the roof of her mouth.

O-kay, then. So she wasn't going to spill her guts. He'd live, even if the disappointment needled at him. "Are you staying in Columbus?"

"No. I'm just visiting my aunt for the summer. I'll probably go back to New York. I'm taking the bar exam there in July. That's where I'm from."

The real estate mogul in him kicked in. "Whereabouts?"

She hesitated. "Manhattan. And Long Island."

Oh, she was funny with her vague answers. Clearly he was dealing with a pampered princess who felt guilty that Daddy's pockets had been so deep. "Whereabouts?" he asked again.

This time she glared, but the wry curl of her lips softened the effect. "Park Avenue and Sag Harbor, if you must know."

He tried not to laugh. "Ah. Low-rent districts. That's a shame."

"Moving on," she said firmly. "What do you do?"

What did he do?

Well, after graduating from Duke, he discovered a lifelong betrayal and, as a result, had a major break from his so-called family. This led to a downward spiral, which in turn led to too much partying and trouble with Johnny Law. After being wrongfully accused and betrayed by a man he'd thought was a friend (betrayal was a running theme in his life, no doubt), he spent several years in prison for a crime he didn't commit and finally got freed via the Innocence Program and the mercy of a victim who realized, after years of therapy, that he wasn't the one.

Then, after struggling to get his feet back on the ground, including an inglorious period working at a car wash (yeah, that was fun), he'd won a grant from former Governor Beau Taylor's Phoenix Legacies Foundation and started flipping houses. He'd since parlayed that into an empire that kept growing despite the lousy economy.

But he wasn't about to put that into twenty-five words or less.

"I'm a real estate developer."

"Real estate." She gave an exaggerated shiver. "Ooh. Exciting."

His lips twitched, but he resisted giving her the whole grin. He wasn't sure why, other than it seemed crucial not to allow her an opening to worm her way under his skin any more than she already had.

"Are you from Columbus?" she asked.

"Born here, yeah."

She snorted. "Did anyone ever tell you that getting you to answer questions was like pulling hen's teeth? Where do you live now?"

"Atlanta."

"So what brings you here? Just the gala?"

Now they were circling a whole big area he didn't want to get anywhere near. So he deflected. "Yeah. And a little, ah, family business. Nosy much?"

"You should talk."

He couldn't deny his keen curiosity about every minute detail of her life, nor could he take his eyes off her. She had a real thing going on there, what with the rapt interest, as though he were the only man in the world who fascinated her, and the vulnerability, as though he could lead her around by the nose if he felt like bothering.

Only, he didn't think it was a thing, and he ought to know. You didn't emerge from the penitentiary intact without being a shrewd judge of character and knowing who you could turn your back on in the shower, and who you couldn't.

If she had half an ounce of sense, she'd stay far away from him.

Hell, if he had a quarter ounce of sense, he'd vacate this terrace now, but sense was apparently thin on the ground tonight, and he didn't want to leave her.

But what was he doing? Where did he think this was going?

Nowhere, that's where.

So he got up even though his limbs felt heavy and resistant, ignored the bright hope shining in her eyes, put his empty dessert bowl on the ledge next to his empty wine goblet and started on his way.

"I need to go," he said. "Have a good night."

Her face fell. "Can't you stay for a minute?"

"No."

"Don't you even want to know my name?"

He hesitated.

Know her name? Didn't she get it? He wanted to know her name, her favorite color, her date of birth and how she liked her eggs at breakfast. He wanted to unravel all the secrets of her body. Most of all, he wanted to know what she'd seen in him that made her approach him when so many people in his life had written him off.

Yeah, he wanted, and the subtle glow of longing in her face, which was partially hidden behind several windblown curls, damn sure wasn't helping.

"Your name?" he asked stupidly.

"It's Arianna. Smith."

This time, finally, he had to laugh. "Arianna? I should have known. You don't look like a Sue, and with brothers named Antonios and Alessandro—"

"It's Greek for 'most holy.'"

"Yeah. I should've known that, too."

"Why?"

The smile slipped away from him, but the words wouldn't shut the hell up. "Because you look like an angel."

She stilled. When she spoke again, her voice was filled with a new huskiness that wound him up tight. "Is someone waiting for you?"

"No."

"Then why can't we spend a little time together?"

Good question. At the moment, he couldn't remember. Something about his agenda and there being no room for a woman in his life, but neither consideration seemed any more immediate than the atmospheric conditions on the planet Mercury. Nothing but this was important—nothing but her.

"It's just—"

"Am I bothering you?"

Yeah, she was, but not in the way she feared. She made him hot and bothered. Intrigued and bothered. She had him on a hook and he didn't particularly want to get free.

"No." He hated admitting it, but he couldn't keep the truth locked up because it burrowed right under the gate like a gopher hopped up on speed. "But I need to know—why me?"

That got her. She dropped her gaze and shook her head. "You'll laugh."

"No, I won't."

"It doesn't make sense."

"Tell me anyway."

He waited, studying the top of her head, watching the sleek black hair flutter in the breeze. They'd gotten closer somehow, probably because he couldn't resist the slow drift of his body toward hers, and he could smell the light flowers of her perfume and, underneath that, the warmth of her clean skin.

Seconds passed. Then she met his gaze again, and understanding shone so bright in her eyes it nearly made his heart stop.

"Because. When I saw you looking at me earlier, I thought, 'He needs me. He doesn't want to, but he does.'"

Jesus. That wasn't what he'd expected.

"So I came to find you."

There was nothing he could say to that, no denial he could manage with a straight face. Because he did need her. Their ten minutes in the moonlight had brought more sunshine to his life than he'd known in years. He didn't like it—she was right about that, his brilliant little Yale Law graduate—but that didn't mean he could ignore it. He'd been in the dark for too long. He needed the sun for as long as he could have it.

Reaching out, he smoothed the hair back from her face so he could keep those eyes in view. They crinkled at the edges, and he felt something deep inside ease up as a little more light crept into his life, a little more hope.

"What's your name?" she asked.

For the first time in years, the wrong name came to his lips: his real name, Joshua. He didn't know why, but it seemed inappropriate to tell her anything else. But of course, Joshua had died long ago, and a little moonlight and romance weren't going to resurrect him.

"Dawson."

"Dawson," she echoed, trying it out for size, and her voice saying it was better than a John Coltrane sax solo. "Can you stay a little longer, Dawson?"

"Yeah." No hesitation this time. "I can do that."

Chapter 2

The delicious moment stretched between them, but Arianna had already discovered that almost everything about this man struck her as delicious. His grumpy wariness, his wounded brown eyes behind frameless glasses. His head full of thick, short, perfectly groomed black dreadlocks, and his pouty lips that were downturned in a perpetual suspicious sulk. The slashing heaviness of his black brows and the glowing walnut of his skin. His commanding height, the breadth of his shoulders and the severity of his suit, all of which made him as dangerously sexy as a siren calling a sailor to his doom from her rocky perch.

He reminded her of a trained grizzly who'd accidentally caught his paw in a trap and now no longer trusted humans. There was, she suspected, a teddy bear imprisoned somewhere inside, but she'd have to slay a thousand dragons to get to him. But, man, she wanted to get to him. Because Dawson made her hot enough to melt her way into the center of a glacier.

Too bad that wasn't the worst of it. He touched her, and that was trickier than mere sexual desire. Later—much later—she'd have to give that some thought. For now, she just wanted him to stick around for a while.

But he'd already backed up a step or two and dropped his hand, and she could feel a moat opening up between them.

Couldn't have that.

So she laughed, both because he was funny in his sulkiness and because it seemed to disarm him so badly, and asked something she'd been wondering.

"You don't smile much, do you?"

This, naturally, produced a full-fledged frown. "I smile."

"Not very much. Bad teeth?"

That got him. Snorting with a grudging laugh that revealed the flash of perfect, strong white teeth, he looked across the lawn toward the house and shoved his hands deep into his pockets. Wow. That was worth the wait. One little smile stripped all that suspicion away and left him dimpled and charming.

She stared at him, her breath spiking. More. She wanted more of that.

Unfortunately, he seemed to catch himself. Maybe he allocated himself only three smiles per day, or maybe it was that each smile could only last for two seconds. Whatever. The smile faded away, leaving him with his default expression: serious.

"See?" he said. "A smile."

"Did it hurt?"

The laughter came a little quicker this time, a little easier. As though his body were flexing out-of-shape muscles and getting stronger with each repetition. Even so, he didn't let it last long.

"You should be happy now. Two smiles in a row."

"Two incredible smiles," she agreed. "Gone too soon."

It would've been nice to keep this in the area of meaningless flirtation, but this seemed important, as though basic understanding of this one point was essential to really getting him. And, more than anything, she wanted to really get him.

They stared at each other, another of those tension-filled moments that sent goose pimples racing over flesh that suddenly felt over-sensitized and alert. He was somehow closer again, and she'd leaned toward him, her hands planted on the ledge for support. His faint clean scent, something dizzying that reminded her of sunshine, water and the raw earthiness of a pine forest after a summer shower, made her want to wrap her arms and legs around him and press her face to his neck.

"What do you want, Arianna?"

That was easy. "I want to know why you're so serious and what I could do to get you to have an easy conversation with me. I want to know what you do for fun when you're not trying to conquer the world."

His brows came together in unmistakable surprise.

"That's right, isn't it? You're out to conquer the world. But why? I want you to tell me. And I want to make you laugh again, because you have a great laugh."

His comeback took a minute. "That's quite a list. Anything else?"

"That's it for now."

"Most people start with asking about pets and hobbies, Arianna."

She shrugged. "Why waste time? I like to cut to

the chase. But if you have a pet you want to tell me about..."

"No pets."

"And no hobbies, either. Right?"

This shrewd assessment seemed to disturb him, because his face darkened. Still, he tried to joke it away. "It takes a lot of time to conquer the world."

"No doubt."

"You come on like a ton of bricks. You ever think about being subtle?"

Ton of bricks? She'd been called worse. Aunt Arnetta Warner, for one, went into daily spasms of horror about Arianna's directness, among other things. The poor woman had spent the first week or so of summer trying to remake Arianna into her vision of Southern gentility, but it was far too late for that. Arianna had already grown into her own woman. This last year had proven that, if nothing else.

"I could be subtle, yeah," she agreed. "But if I'd been subtle tonight, you'd be gone and I'd be here by myself, eating two bowls of mousse and looking around for another one. That would've been sad, wouldn't it? Because we like each other."

He hesitated. She could feel him considering various denials and evasions, trying them on for size and seeing which ones might fly. In the end, he just admitted it, and that grudging admission felt like the pot of gold at the end of the rainbow.

"Yeah." His voice was huskier now, his gaze a little more intent. His absolute and unwavering attention surrounded her, edging everything else away from her vision until only he was left. "We like each other."

Those four words shouldn't have made her this unreasonably happy, but they did. Everything within her smiled, but her mouth couldn't manage the gesture, not with him staring at her like that.

Tone it back, girl, she told herself sternly. *You're not ready for a relationship, and this is only flirting anyway.*

Only it wasn't. Definitely not on her part, and she'd bet that this…thing between them, whatever it was, was new to him, too.

The air between them held all sorts of promise, like a cloudy summer sky in those last few seconds before the first drops of rain fell. She opened her mouth, waiting for her chatterbox instincts to kick in again so they could resume their mostly one-sided conversation, but words ran and hid.

And still he stared at her, inches away, his hands in his pockets.

"Cat got your tongue?" he murmured.

Her lips worked, trapped somewhere between a slow smile and an answer to his question. "I'm not sure. This has never happened to me before."

"What?"

They both knew he wasn't asking about her sudden silence.

"Any of this," she said.

It was true. This last year, she'd been so celibate she probably qualified for re-virginization. Back in the day, she'd had the usual amount of collegiate sexual experience, some of which involved alcohol. That being the case, she knew that alcohol could lower her inhibitions, which were well below sea level at this point. But she'd only had half a glass of champagne about two hours ago, so she couldn't blame being drunk for the unreasonable chemistry she felt right now.

Nor could she blame a generalized horniness for this

attraction, because she and her battery-operated boyfriend got along quite well, thank you very much.

No.

That left only one conclusion, reluctant as she was to come to it: this was all about Dawson, his effect on her and hers on him.

"What now?" His eyes were heavy lidded, his voice the lowest whisper.

God. She couldn't even speak.

Her face was hot, her breasts heavy. Between her legs, she felt the slick wetness of her body's response to him, the insistent clench of inner muscles.

It was inevitable, then. This. Them. Tonight. Now.

"You could kiss me," she said.

He hesitated, studying her face and deciding. She would have told him not to fight it, but her voice had left the building.

For the first time in what seemed like hours, he looked away from her face, to her bare shoulder, which was pressed up near her jaw line. Taking all the time in the world, he pulled his hand out of his pocket and slid his long, neat fingers up her arm, to the point that held his absolute attention.

Then he circled with his thumb, leaned in and pressed a kiss to her shoulder. A long, wet, scorching kiss.

"Oh, God." Her heavy head fell back and she stared up at the black sky, seeing both those stars and the ones he'd made flash across her vision. The air could no longer get to her heaving lungs, and she had one millisecond to wonder what was happening here, what they'd unleashed, but then it was too late for thinking and he was nipping at her neck and easing his body between her legs. "God."

His other hand came out of his pocket, and everything happened at once. His hungry, searching mouth ran back and forth over that sweet tendon—there, God, right there—and continued on its way up her exposed throat, across her cheek, to his final destination: her lips.

He waited there, hovering just long enough to make her want to scream with frustration. Her arms went around his shoulders, anchoring him closer between her thighs, and his hands slipped over the silk of her dress, to her butt, dragging her up against a heart-stopping erection that he ground against her. Then they went to her breasts, stroking and kneading.

He kissed her, silencing her cries. His skilled mouth claimed her, sucking and biting his way deep inside, his tongue plunging and retreating. Relentless. He tasted like chocolate, wine and heaven, and she wanted to gorge until she passed out with it, and then she wanted to gorge again.

Without warning, he broke the kiss and leaned his forehead against hers, panting. They stayed like that for several breathless beats, shocked with the power of their connection, and then he pulled back just enough to study her with eyes that were glazed and glittering with desire behind those glasses.

"Yes or no, Arianna?"

"Y—"

His body shuddered with what was probably a restrained combination of relief and lust—it looked like he almost smiled—but then his hands on her breasts loosened a little, robbing her of the pleasure she needed, and his thumbs stopped circling her nipples.

"Think about it," he warned.

He was right, of course. She should think about this, come to the sensible decision and stop before things got out of hand. Her life was unsettled, and she'd just come off the worst year she'd ever known. She wasn't ready for a relationship, and this man was a complete stranger who, for all she knew, could be on a day pass from the local mental institution.

So she should say no. That was the smart thing. *No.* Do it.

She opened her mouth.

"Yes," she said, and her whole heart was in that one word. "Yes."

Chapter 3

"Come to my hotel," he said, his voice dark now, thick with passion.

Hotel? Did he think she could wait that long without bursting into flames of spontaneous combustion? The cottage was much closer, but there was no way the two of them could slip past hundreds of people, especially her sharp-eyed aunt Arnetta and Bishop, her extra pair of eyes, unnoticed.

She looked wildly around, saying a quick but fervent prayer of thanks that their little spot on the faraway terrace was dark and secluded enough to hide what they were doing.

"No," she said. "Greenhouse. Hurry."

"Greenhouse?"

He seemed bewildered for half a second but then looked around, saw the greenhouse behind them and came up to speed. His face grim with determination, he snatched her off the ledge just as she was, arms and legs wrapped around him in a stranglehold, and swung her around with what felt like the strength of three or four men. Holding her in a death grip, as though she might try to sneak away while his attention was diverted—yeah, right, as if—he strode the rest of the way down the path and banged through the greenhouse door and into the humid warmth inside.

It was dark, with only the sketchy moonlight filtering through the panes of glass to light their way. Luckily, she'd been there several times since she'd arrived and knew exactly where they could go.

"There's a bench," she said, pointing. "By the fountain."

He was already halfway there, led by the steady trickling of water. Multitasking with those clever fingers as he went, he ran his hands up her bare thighs, to her butt, and went to work on her lacy black bikinis. Then he lowered her onto her back on the padded bench with all the care in the world, as though he'd be graded on gentleness later, and sat beside her, stripping the panties down her legs and off past her heels. When that was done, he worked his way between her thighs, exposing her, resting one of her legs up on the back of the bench and the other across his lap.

He sat for a minute, studying her in the darkness, his eyes the only gleam of light in this thrilling inner world, as he shrugged his way out of his jacket. She tracked his every move, her lungs straining with the effort to breathe and her skin all but quivering for his touch.

She wished she could see him better. She wished he was inside her, *now.* Most of all, she wished this night would go on forever because she knew, already felt it in the marrow of her bones, that this one time would never be enough.

"Dawson," she said, opening her arms to him, "come here."

The raw need in her voice galvanized him, and he stretched out over her on the cramped wooden bench, creeping his way up her body, pressing his face to her breasts for a quick nuzzle. Then he cupped her face in his strong hands and gave her a long kiss that was... aaah, yesss...deep, urgent and unbearably sweet. Then he returned his attention to her body, slipping his fingers along the curve of one breast and under her dress.

"Yes or no?" he whispered.

"Yes."

He worked the zipper and eased the straps and bodice down over her arms, baring her to the balmy air. Her puckering nipples had barely bounced back into place, before he claimed one and then the other with his mouth. He squeezed them together and suckled, rhythmically and hard, his swirling tongue doing unspeakable things to her, until her hips writhed and her cries drowned out the trickling fountain.

Crooning with unmistakable pleasure, a purely male sound that came from deep in his chest, he slid lower, past the bodice and skirt of her gown, both of which were now bunched up at her waist, and stopped at the V between her legs.

She went still, the wait making her crazed. His hot mouth latched on to the meaty part of one thigh, sucked it deep into his mouth and scraped it with his teeth as he let go.

The pleasure collected all over her body and pooled in her throat, all but choking her. And her breathing? Forget it. As he turned to her other thigh, the rippling contractions began deep in her belly, gathering strength.

And that was before he licked her core—one long,

leisurely swipe of his tongue that made her writhe to get away and writhe to get closer.

"Dawson," she gasped. "Don't do this to me—"

He lifted his head and spoke in that implacable voice, digging his fingers into her hips to keep her in place. "Yes or no?"

"Dawson—"

"Yes or no?"

A hysteria-tinged burst of laughter bubbled out of her, and she shook her head even as she stretched out, stared at the silvery panes of glass overhead and reached up to grab one of the bench's wooden slats to anchor herself against what he was about to do.

"Arianna?" he whispered.

The rising impatience in his voice drove her on.

"Yes."

That dark head lowered again, and this time the rumbling laughter was his. His clever mouth zeroed in on her engorged nub for another lick or two, a swirl, and that was all it took. She came, her body shuddering and then going rigid, her ecstasy ringing through the greenhouse on a single high note of astonishment.

He rose up over her again, his unforgiving weight pressing her hard against the bench's seat. She didn't care. Raising her sluggish arms, trying to reconnect herself to something sturdy after that soaring pleasure, she thrust her hands deep into his dreadlocks and brought his mouth down to hers. The kiss was urgent but controlled, his hair thick and softer than the Egyptian cotton of her sheets at home.

"Was that good?" he murmured against her lips.

"So good." The words were slurred because she could hardly speak when he'd turned her body to molten gold. "So good."

"Are we done?"

Done? Oh, he was funny.

"Not by a long shot."

She felt his grin before he slipped away and sat up, heaving her along with him. Straddling his lap, she hiked up her skirt, enjoying the slither of the silk against her skin. His hands went to her butt, kneading and drawing her closer, until they were face-to-face and the intimacy of staring into his dark eyes was almost more than what they'd just shared.

"Arianna."

The way he said it—equally tender and rueful, as though he wasn't sure what they were doing here, with each other, like this, but he was going to go with it—sent shivers skittering up her spine.

"Yes?"

He reached between her legs, stroking her swollen wet flesh until she was just this side of insanity. He watched her the whole time, absorbing all her reactions, every sigh, blink and involuntary twist of her face.

Then, still staring at her, he moved his hands to his belt and worked on that. The slow slide of his zipper was next—too slow, as though he wanted to give her plenty of warning and opportunity to stop the proceedings in their tracks.

Stop? Not in a million years.

"I have a condom," he told her, freeing himself.

What? Condom?

Condom! Good thinking. She knew there was something she'd been forgetting in the thrill of his hands all over her body.

"Thank God."

He grinned, then put his hand on the back of her head

to bring her in for another kiss, a rough, quick one this time. "Is that a yes?"

"It's a yes."

He didn't waste any time. Fishing a red packet out of his pocket, he opened the thing and worked it on. She tried to stay out of his way and give him the space he needed to get the job done, but that was impossible when she couldn't keep her hands off him. Trembling with excitement, she palmed his face and kissed him. Forehead, eyes, cheeks—everything she could reach and nuzzle and taste.

And then she came to his mouth again, just as he lifted her to her knees and positioned himself beneath her, poised and straining with the need to slide inside her.

She paused, taking a second to stare at his amazing face and wonder why he'd been sent into her life now, when she'd least expected it, to affect her like this.

"Dawson," she whispered, licking her way between his lips.

They kissed and kissed, and the tension built, threatening to pulse outward in a single wave and shatter the glass all around them. For the first time all night, she felt a flicker of fear, and it had nothing to do with having sex with a man she'd just met.

Sensing this, he broke the kiss and looked up at her, concern knitting those heavy brows. He must have seen something in her face, because he reined himself in until she felt his restraint in every iron-hard muscle beneath her.

"What is it?"

She knew he would stop if she asked, but she didn't want him to stop. She just wanted him to understand.

"If this is going to be the only time between us, just tell me, okay?" God. She hoped she didn't sound too clingy; few things killed a promising erection like a needy woman.

"If you tell me the truth right now, I promise not to get my heart broken, and I won't chase after you or anything, and I'll be fine. But I just...please tell me, okay?"

"The only time?" He blinked, looking as though he was having trouble translating what she'd just said from English into a language he understood. "With you?" He paused, cocking his head to consider her. "Have you lost your mind?"

"No." She was just insanely vulnerable where he was concerned.

Unsmiling, he took his length and stroked her with it, easing her down just a little, until her body began to relax and prepare for some of the stretching she'd need to do to accommodate him.

"You're going to have to find a place in your life for me for a while, Arianna," he told her. "Got it?"

"Got it," she whispered.

"And while we're having this little heart-to-heart—that man from the breakup you didn't want to tell me about. He's not coming back for you, is he? Because I may have to kill him."

In Dawson's arms like this, it was hard to believe there'd ever been a Carter, or anyone else, or ever could be. "It's over. Way over."

"Good." His lips curled into a slow smile. Grazing her mouth again, he slid another inch inside her, and they both gasped at the friction. "Yes or no?"

"Yes."

With that, she impaled herself until he was so deep inside her it felt as though nothing could ever separate them.

Chapter 4

Arianna sat on the bench and buckled her strappy sandal. Dawson, who'd already straightened his clothes and gotten rid of the condom, watched her, searching his memory banks. He wasn't aware of taking off her shoes, but he'd had his hands over every part of her that he could reach, so it was entirely possible.

He studied her, endlessly fascinated. At the moment, his attention was riveted to the moonlit gleam of her leg where her skirt fell away, and to the curve of her breasts as she bent at the waist, and, hell, to everything else about her. He suspected this woman would have him under her spell—and it was a spell, because no other woman had ever affected him like this; not even close—for some indeterminate period yet to come, but he didn't want to think about those ramifications right now.

Right now they needed to address Arianna's growing embarrassment and the heat from her face, which had to be glowing red even if he couldn't see it clearly in the dark. He had his hand buried deep in the thick hair at her nape, massaging her. For comfort, he told himself, but whether he was comforting her or himself was open to debate.

Either way, he couldn't stop touching her.

Finally the elaborate shoe-reattachment ritual was finished and there was nothing else she could do to postpone the moment when she had to look at him. Her dress was arranged, her hair fluffed. Nothing to do now but figure out where they went from here.

Like he knew.

She leaned back against the bench and they sat, silent, floundering and surprised by this turn of events. God knew he couldn't have foreseen any of this when he put on his suit tonight.

"You okay?" he finally asked.

She ducked her head and grinned, risking a sidelong look at him that had a hard, tight knot of lust coiling in his gut. Again.

"I think you know that I'm much better than okay."

Good. This confirmation made him want to puff out his chest and pound it, to tilt back his head and roar with satisfaction until the sound echoed all around the world. He resisted the urge but couldn't prevent a quick curl of his lips.

What now?

The two of them had vaulted into uncharted territory tonight. He felt like an early explorer who'd reached the edge of the known world, where the map ended and the legend read Here Be Dragons. He didn't like the unknown, but on the other hand, he liked her uncharacteristic shyness even less.

"So why won't you look at me?"

She ran a hand through her hair, struggling for words. "It's just that…I'm not sure what happened here."

"Neither am I."

"There's a lot we don't know about each other."

Ain't that the truth? "I know."

"You wouldn't know this about me, but I've never—"

"Don't." Tightening his grip on her nape, he pulled her in for a hard kiss. "Don't," he said again when they pulled apart, both breathless, and she tried to keep talking.

He couldn't stand it. The idea of her doing what they'd just done with some other man made him…whoa. Already he could feel his blood pressure ticking higher, his pulse rushing in his ears. He didn't want to go there, didn't even want the thought to fully form. It might make his brain implode.

And double standards of any kind, even his own, pissed him off, so they wouldn't go down this road, not even a step or two.

Besides, his screaming instincts told him that Arianna didn't give herself lightly, not to anyone. Which scared the hell out of him, because what did she think she saw in him that made him worthy of such an honor? Whatever it was surely didn't exist.

"You don't owe me any explanations," he told her.

"Of course not, but I need to tell you—"

"Arianna. Knock it off. I know you had a life before tonight."

And so did he, not that now was the time to get into it.

She started to say something else, but he stroked her under the chin to soften his words. "Anyway, don't you want to resume your interrogation? You haven't asked about my zodiac sign yet, or what size shoe I wear."

She tried to glare, but her eyes crinkled at the corners

and she dimpled, ruining the whole effect. When she gave up, tossed all that thick hair over her shoulder and flashed him the full, glorious smile, he felt something inside him turn over, and turn over hard.

The funny thing was, he didn't even want to fight it.

"What about your favorite magazines?" she asked. "Why don't we start there?"

He laughed, and then she laughed, and then suddenly nothing about this whole situation was even partially funny. He was here at Heather Hill for a reason that had nothing to do with her. His plans couldn't include her. Even if they could, she was so far above him she might have been the Hope Diamond, orbiting on the International Space Station, while he was a slug buried deep in the earth.

Arianna exuded class and money, the kind of breezy joie de vivre that told him she'd never been hungry a day in her life, never struggled for money, status or basic fairness, never wondered who she was or if she was loved.

And he?

He was an innocent ex-con who didn't have jack or shit, other than a few dollars in the bank. Well, make that a lot of dollars.

Arianna may as well try to strike up a relationship with a great white shark as with him. It'd have more of a chance of success. The knowledge spurred him to grim honesty, because God knew she'd never done anything in her life to deserve him.

"You can do so much better than me."

He saw her sudden frown in the darkness, the flattening of her fine brows into an intransigent line that seemed like a clear warning: she wanted to kick his ass for saying something so stupid. But at the last second she changed course and shrugged, laughing at him.

"Oh, I know," she said on an exaggerated sigh. "I'm only here out of pity."

He snorted. "Pity works for me."

She kissed him again and then got up, shook out her skirt and took his hand to pull him up, too. "We should get back to the party. I'm starving."

A sudden flare of panic caught him by the throat. He didn't want her to leave and didn't want to go back to the party. Inside this greenhouse was a private sanctuary where a woman like her could belong with a man like him. Out there, reality crouched in hiding, waiting to knock him back to his rightful place at the first opportunity.

Tightening his grip on her hand, he swung her around, reeled her back into his arms and wished he could suspend time. While she was in here, she didn't have to know who he was or the crimes he'd been accused of or the world's low opinion of him. Out there, disaster could only follow.

He wrapped her up and kissed her, absorbing her peep of surprise into his mouth and running his hands all over those delicious curves, again, imprinting everything about her and this interlude. Then he let her go.

"What was that for?" she gasped, cheeks flushed with pleasure.

"Remember this," he said urgently. "Don't forget."

That wide-eyed gaze held him. "Do you think I could?"

God, he hoped not.

Nodding, satisfied for now, he opened the door for her and they walked outside into the night air, which had cooled since they last felt it. They held hands, saying nothing, and meandered back up the path to their terrace.

Across the way, high on the hill, the main house was still lit like a city skyline, every window glowing bright, and candles and lanterns flickered along the paths and in the various gardens and courtyards. The music had switched since they'd been gone, and now a live singer hidden somewhere sang—no kidding—"Strangers in the Night."

"Did you try the pasta bar?" she asked, resting her head on his shoulder.

He thought back. "Was that the one in the music room?"

"No, that was the sushi bar. The pasta bar was—oh, is that your phone?"

It was, vibrating in his pocket. They paused at the outer edge of the terrace surrounding the house, where the designer-clothes-wearing, champagne-drinking crowd was starting to get thick again, while he fished it out and glanced at the display.

"Sorry. It's one of my property managers on the West Coast," he told her.

"Oh. Well, why don't you talk to him, and I'll meet you at the pasta bar in the solarium. I'll just see you in a minute."

"Okay," he said, even though he didn't want her out of his sight. It was too soon and she was too precious, but he wasn't the obsessed stalker type, so he dialed it back as much as he could. "See you in a minute."

They both took a step away from each other, but neither wanted to let go. Their arms stretched between them, extending the connection, until Arianna, with that sultry laugh that drove him wild, snatched her cool fingertips from his, waved and went into the house.

The French door shut in his face, but he watched her weave through the crowd until she was gone and the normal emptiness echoed through him.

Loneliness, his old pal. Showing up to keep him company. Again.

Looking down at his phone, he took a couple steps back toward the far end of the terrace and searched for a quieter spot with better reception. It was the wrong place to multitask, though, because he plowed straight into someone.

"Sorry," he began, glancing up. "I didn't see—"

Jesus. It was Franklin Bishop.

They both froze, as though they'd run headlong into an electrified brick wall.

Dawson had thought he was prepared for this moment, but readiness turned out to be an illusion. All the old emotions, the ones he thought he'd beaten into submission, came flooding back: Anger. Outrage. The bitter sting of betrayal.

The old guy wasn't doing too good, either. After the initial surprise, he staggered back a step, a weathered hand going to his temple. His mouth opened and closed…once…twice…but no words.

The years had done their work on him. He looked spry for his age, true, wiry and smoothly brown-skinned, with only the white-on-white hair and dark spots across his forehead to give him away. But the bottom line was that time hadn't stood still for any of them, and this was an old man who'd be staring down the end of his life before too much longer.

And that was a kick right in Dawson's gut.

Time to go.

"Excuse me." Dawson tried to edge past him, not inside to Arianna, but to the front of the house, to his car, to escape. He would get Arianna's number somehow and call her later, or find her tomorrow. He had resources; he could do that. She'd be pissed, yeah, but he'd make her understand that something had come up.

What he couldn't do was stand here with Franklin Bishop and watch the dawning horror spread over his face. He took a step, but Bishop's hand lashed out, gripping him by the forearm, stopping him.

"Joshua," he said, his voice deepened with age and hoarse with emotion, but otherwise the same as Dawson remembered it.

Dawson snatched free, snarling as he brushed past. "Joshua's dead."

"No." Bishop tried to keep pace, his voice rising with desperation. "Son," he called, *"please."*

Dawson paused, the years of accumulated ugliness twisting his lips into a sneer. "You don't have a son. And I sure as hell don't have a father."

Where did he go?

Arianna slumped in the wingback chair nearest the open French doors overlooking the pool, nursed her hot chocolate and hated life. She hated the stupid, bright sunshiny day outside, and she hated the happy little roses in the garden, with their velvety pink-and-yellow petals and heavy fragrance. Her hot chocolate was too sweet, and she hated that. Over on the far wall above the mantel, a portrait of Uncle Reynolds glared down at her, and she wished she could toss her hot chocolate in his haughty face. She also hated herself for (a) wasting the final hours of last night's party desperately searching for a man who'd walked out on her without a word, (b) feeling devastated about it and (c) losing sleep over it.

Most of all, she hated Dawson. For doing this to her.

Although, to be fair, had he really done anything to her?

Other than making her foolish heart flutter and screwing her senseless, that is?

No. He hadn't.

She finished the last sip of her hot chocolate and stared moodily at the dark dregs at the bottom, accepting the brutal truth about herself and what she'd done last night. It wasn't pretty.

Why was she making him the bad guy? He hadn't done anything other than accept her oh-so-enthusiastic offer of no-holds-barred, no-questions-asked sex. What man wouldn't? Should she blame him for that? No. He hadn't followed her. He hadn't flirted with her. Hell, he'd even tried to leave without learning her name.

How much clearer could he have been?

I'm not interested, dummy. That's what he'd been saying. And here she was, so unspeakably dumb that she'd not only not gotten the message, but she'd gleefully had sex in a greenhouse with a man whose last name she didn't even know.

Brilliant.

Dummy.

Slamming the cup down on the side table—Aunt Arnetta would throw a fit later because what if, God forbid, a moisture ring turned up on her precious mahogany?—Arianna heaved herself up and went to stare out at the pool, seeing nothing in particular. Some stupid family meeting would be starting soon, but for now she had a few good minutes left to sulk, and she planned to make the most of the time.

The thing was, why hadn't Dawson just told her the truth? That's why she was so upset right now, the real reason she'd cried last night and felt like she'd been backed over by an eighteen-wheeler with snow chains on the tires. She'd asked him whether they were just having a one-time thing, and he'd said no. Why'd he lie? He'd had her by then; she'd been so desperate by that point to feel him moving inside her that she wouldn't have minded if he'd confessed to being a brain-chomping zombie.

But what did she expect? That was a man for you: wall-to-wall empty promises. He'd looked her straight in the face and made up some pretty nonsense about being a part of her life for a while.

Huh. Maybe that was the problem. She should have asked him to define "a while." He could have told her that to him it only meant long enough to ejaculate, and then she'd've known exactly what she was getting.

Oh, come on. Who was she fooling? She had known. Please. When in the history of life had any sort of worthwhile relationship evolved from a sexual encounter within an hour of meeting someone? Never, that's when. Dawson had only done what he apparently thought, in his twisted, stupid little male mind, was the right thing—may he die a thousand excruciating deaths and his black soul burn in the hottest fires of hell forever—and let her down easy.

"Arianna?"

Not that she'd thought they'd get married and live happily ever after, or anything ridiculous like that—

"Arianna?"

But she had expected to share a bowl of pasta or something with him. Maybe get to know each other a little better and see what happened. Was that too much to hope?

"Arianna!"

Arianna jumped, unwillingly blasted out of her thoughts by her aunt's insistent voice. "What?" she said ungraciously.

Arnetta Warner, her aunt on her mother's side, gave

Arianna the Look, which was a genteel Southern frown that consisted of slightly lowered brows and pursed lips. "My goodness," she drawled. "I've never seen such a collection of sourpusses. Is there something in the water today? What's gotten into all of you?"

Arianna was about to ask for an explanation, because surely no one else in the house could feel as bad as she currently did, but then she saw Bishop and did a triple take.

He trailed along in Aunt Arnetta's wake, pushing the breakfast cart, which was weighed down with coffee- and teapots, pastries and who knew what else. He was starched and pressed as usual, with his white dress shirt and dark slacks as dapper as ever, but his shoulders and eyes drooped, and she wondered whether the cart was the only thing holding him up.

"Bishop?" Worry crept over Arianna's skin. Bishop, she already knew from her brief time here at Heather Hill, was the rock, the touchstone of sanity, in a house full of oversized personalities and fragile egos. If something was wrong with Bishop, then something was seriously wrong. "You okay?"

"'Course I'm okay." Steering the cart next to the coffee table, he smiled, winked and put some more spring in his step. "Just a little tired after the big party. You want some more hot chocolate?"

This was not convincing, especially now that he was close enough for her to see the grayish tinge to his brown skin, as though he'd soon be regurgitating whatever he'd eaten this morning. She was about to press the issue, but he waited, smiling with such an air of determined avoidance that she couldn't say one more word. Instead, she passed him her empty cup.

"Thanks." She and Aunt Arnetta exchanged discreet

sidelong looks, silently agreeing that they were concerned about him and would discuss the matter later. "That'd be great."

Bishop poured the steaming hot chocolate with all the serenity of Gandhi during his daily meditation and handed it back to her. "You enjoy the party?"

"Yep," Arianna said.

The false note in her voice flipped the switch on in Bishop's eagle eye, and he stopped arranging plates and napkins long enough to swing his sharpened gaze back around to her. "You sure? Your eyes look a little bleary to me."

"That's what I thought," Aunt Arnetta chimed in.

Uh-oh. She sooo did not need an interrogation from these two this early in the morning. Mirroring Bishop's forced smile right back at him, she crinkled her brows, trying to look bewildered by the topic.

"Of course I'm okay. Why wouldn't I be?"

Aunt Arnetta sat on the sofa, arranged a napkin over her tailored gray slacks and accepted a cup of tea from Bishop. "And where did you go last night? I wanted to introduce you to a young man from a nice family. He's a second-year student at Yale Law, and he'd be just perfect for—"

"Oh, Lord." Not this again.

Aunt Arnetta blinked with all the innocence of a puppy opening its eyes to the world for the first time. Like they'd never discussed this topic before. Like she had no idea about Arianna's stance on things like marriage and nice young men.

"Is there a problem, dear? And do stand up straight. You're slouching."

Arianna, who had in fact been slouching against the tall back of a chair, sipping her hot chocolate, took this opportunity to drive a couple of points home and kill two birds with one stone. Straightening with the deportment of a debutante in training with a book on her head, she swept around to the front of the chair, making sure to swish the skirt of her sundress like a Southern belle, perched on the edge and crossed her legs at the ankle.

Aunt Arnetta smiled with approval.

Then Arianna slouched back into the chair and propped her feet on the ottoman.

Aunt Arnetta froze, her arm suspended halfway to the platter of bran muffins.

Bishop choked back a snort of laughter.

"The thing you need to understand about me, Aunt Arnetta," Arianna said, "is that I'm really independent. I don't need to be told how to sit or stand or walk, and I definitely don't need to be told about nice young men from good families. I can find my own boyfriends, thank you very much."

"Nonsense." Aunt Arnetta selected a muffin. "Left to your own devices, you'd probably turn up with a boy with a motorcycle and a—" she shuddered at the mere thought, her thin shoulders shifting inside her blue-and-white plaid Chanel jacket "—tattoo."

Arianna scowled and tried too late to hide the scowl behind a big bite of a hastily snatched spice scone. Dawson No-Last-Name appeared in her mind's eye again, commandeering her thoughts. Because he had a tattoo—she'd seen the edges of it on his neck above his tailored shirt last night, and she'd meant to ask him what it was. If it hadn't been so dark in the greenhouse last night, she'd've seen it.

Now she never would.

Nor would she ever see his bare chest in all its considerable glory, or his toned belly, or his...well, she wouldn't go lower than that. The bottom line was that he'd captured her imagination, turned her body out and then evaporated like a vampire into the mist.

Goodbye and good riddance.

"I like tattoos," she said sullenly.

"That's the problem, dear," Aunt Arnetta said.

"What's the problem?" asked a new voice.

Andrew Warner strode into the room, with Eric Warner close on his heels. Suddenly things were looking up, and Arianna had to smile. Where those two went mischief followed, the way day follows night.

As Aunt Arnetta's grandchildren (sort of), Andrew and Eric were Arianna's cousins (she supposed). Here at Heather Hill, it was always best not to examine the family tree in minute detail because you never knew what you'd turn up. Bottom line? Though they were older than she was, closer to her brother Sandro's age, they'd all spent summers together at Arianna's parents' home in the Hamptons, and she loved them like crazy, even when they teased her mercilessly.

The two men were exactly alike and yet totally different. Both were tall and sexy and brought an overload of testosterone with them wherever they went. Both were really smart corporate-tycoon types, and both thought they were in charge of the world. The only thing on earth more alpha than these two was the lead wolf in a pack, or maybe a silverback gorilla. Until it came to the females in their lives, which was the interesting part. Each man was wildly in love with his wife and had a heart bigger than the Alaskan tundra when it came to his family.

On the other hand, Andrew was fair skinned, blue-eyed and stern, while Eric was dark, bright-eyed and easy to smile.

The funny thing was, they ribbed each other relentlessly

and acted like they barely tolerated each other. Meanwhile, whenever they got together—which wasn't that often because Eric lived here in Columbus, which was the headquarters of the family business, WarnerBrands International, while Andrew headed his own company in New York City—they were glued at the hip.

Like now.

One after the other, they shook hands with Bishop, kissed Aunt Arnetta, then Arianna, and then sprawled on the nearest sofa together, their long legs stretching out and taking up way too much space.

"What'd we miss?" Eric grabbed a plate and eyed the treats.

Without a word, Andrew took Eric's plate and commandeered it for his own by putting a croissant on it. "Yeah," he said, piling on the food. "Sounded interesting."

"Help yourself," Eric muttered, then grabbed another plate.

"Aunt Arnetta was just saying I should find a nice man from a good family." Arianna, now at the end of her scone, eyed the muffins. Would one of those be too much? Yeah. She'd better not. "She wants to hook me up with someone like you two, I suppose."

Both Andrew and Eric snorted.

It was a well-known bit of family lore that, before those two met their wives, they'd run through the ladies the way Wile E. Coyote runs through dynamite. Fun was had; women were enjoyed; female hearts were broken. Now, though, they both had kids, which no doubt gave them a different perspective on the dating scene.

"Ah…" Andrew began.

"I don't think you want anyone like us," Eric told Arianna. "Why don't you play the field for a while?"

"That's my point." Arianna eyeballed Aunt Arnetta

to make sure she was getting the message, but the older woman looked smug and undeterred. "I just got out of a relationship and I'm not looking for another one. And being from a—" she made quotation marks with her fingers "—*good family* is no guarantee that a man is worthwhile. Look at these two clowns."

Andrew and Eric, both chewing now, exchanged a look.

"She talking about us?" Andrew questioned, brows lifting.

"Couldn't be," Eric replied.

Enough with the comedy routine. "Where are the womenfolk, Abbott and Costello?" Arianna asked.

"They took the kids to the zoo." Andrew checked his watch. "And our mysterious investor should be here any minute. I want to get this show on the road. I told Viveca I'd try to meet them for lunch."

Aunt Arnetta patted her mouth with a napkin. "I'm still not sure what this meeting is about."

"I'm not quite sure, either," Andrew told her. "All I know is, this real estate developer wanted to speak with us about an opportunity he said we wouldn't want to miss—"

"Oh, please." Aunt Arnetta looked exasperated. "Did he send over a prospectus or anything? Why all the mystery? And why couldn't we do this at the office?"

Andrew shrugged. "His people said he's an old friend of Grandfather's." Even though they'd discovered a couple of years ago that Reynolds Warner, Arnetta's late husband, was actually Andrew's father due to an affair he'd had with Andrew's mother, Andrew still referred to him as "Grandfather." This was probably the easiest thing, given the complex relationships at Heather Hill, which seemed at times like a hotbed of lust and infidelity. "I didn't feel like I should tell him no. And he's got a good reputation, so this could be worthwhile."

"Let's hope so," Aunt Arnetta said.

Bishop topped off Eric's coffee cup, rearranged a couple of things on the cart to his liking and straightened to go. "If everything looks okay," he said to the room at large, "I'll leave you folks to your meeting."

This was the perfect time to slip out. She could hardly spend the day licking her wounds in a roomful of people, could she? Arianna got to her feet and put her plate down. "I'll come with you. I don't want to be in the way."

"What are your plans for the day, dear?" Aunt Arnetta called after her.

A long morning of sulking, followed by reliving every delicious moment of last night's interlude with Dawson the Unknown, punctuated by frequent binges of alcohol and chocolate to ease the pain.

"Nothing in particular. See you." Arianna took Bishop's arm and walked toward the hall door.

Bishop, whose skin color was still a little off, patted her hand and gave her a fond smile. They liked each other, she and Bishop; they were united in their love for Aunt Arnetta and their mutual refusal to let her rule their lives like a communist dictator. Bishop was the kind of fine old gentleman they didn't make anymore, and she really hoped nothing was wrong with him.

"You sure you're okay?" she whispered.

He cocked one grizzled brow at her. "You sure *you're* okay?"

They were both lying about their okay-ness, and they both knew it. That being the case, there was nothing to do but laugh. They were still chuckling when one of the maids bustled into the library and spoke to Aunt Arnetta.

"Mr. Reynolds is here to see you, ma'am."

With that she stepped aside, and someone else walked in, a man, and— *Oh, my God.*

He was tall and broad shouldered, impeccably dressed in a fine dark suit with red tie, a conservative businessman to the core as long as you looked at him from the torso down. The mocking expression in his midnight eyes, however, was a nice, loud "screw you" to the establishment, especially *this* establishment, and his short dreadlocks and tattooed neck only intensified the effect.

He was the perfect combination of the buttoned-down corporate type and the unmitigated bad boy, the perfect addition to the potent masculinity already filling the room, and he stopped Arianna's heartbeat cold.

She froze; Bishop froze; they all froze.

It couldn't be.

But…as the implacable dark gaze behind the rimless glasses swept the room and settled on her, Arianna realized with a room-swaying burst of clarity that her eyes weren't playing nasty tricks on her overwhelmed imagination. This really was Dawson, the man whose hot touch had driven her wild last night.

Only, he hadn't come back for her. Worse. He wasn't happy to see her.

This bitter dose of reality stripped the residual smile off her face.

She wasn't the only one having a tough time right now.

Beside her, Bishop gripped her arm for support, his disbelieving gaze riveted on Dawson as though he'd just seen a long-dead loved one climb from his grave and say hello. His breath turned to a disturbing wheeze. "Joshua?"

Joshua? What? Why was he calling Dawson by the wrong name?

A disbelieving second passed, and then the awful truth hit her: she didn't know one thing about the man she'd made love to last night.

Chapter 5

So much for being ready for this moment, Dawson thought.

Well, he was ready—for most of it.

Having run into Bishop last night, he knew he'd see exactly this drop-jawed horror on the old man's face. And Andrew and Eric hadn't changed even half an iota, so Dawson had known he'd see those thundercloud expressions, all lowered brows, flashing eyes and jutting chins…aaaand yep. There they were.

Arnetta, he'd prepared for. She pretty much had one expression, no matter the occasion: disapproving. She looked disapproving if you broke a window, spilled a drop of water on one of her precious rugs or reappeared in her life after ten years without a word. So, yeah, she looked disapproving now. Dawson felt a moment's pang for what he was about to do to her well-ordered life, because he hated to hurt her.

He'd been ready for all that when he walked back into this room.

The thing he hadn't been ready for was linked arm-in-arm with the old man, as though she was a beloved member of the very family that hated his guts, and she was staring at Dawson with those same brown eyes that had shone so brightly for him last night, sending his world spinning in new directions. Only now those eyes were wide with dismay. Hurt. Humiliation.

"Dawson?" Arianna said.

The intensity in her voice got him. He couldn't tell whether she was mostly hurt or angry because he wasn't who he'd said he was last night.

On the other hand, who the hell was she, and what was she doing here?

And then Arnetta Warner, queen of Heather Hill, came forward and put a protective arm around both Bishop and Arianna, and this simple gesture clicked all the pieces into place for him.

"I'm just visiting my aunt for the summer," Arianna had said last night.

Suddenly he knew: Arianna Smith was a Warner by another name.

Just like him.

Ironic, huh?

And now her aunt, Arnetta the Matriarch, wanted to protect the little princess from him, the Big Bad Wolf. Too bad Auntie hadn't been on the job last night, but better late than never. This little meeting was the reminder that both he and Arianna needed: they had no place in each other's lives, regardless of whatever unexpected magic had passed between them in that greenhouse.

What he was about to do—what he had to do—would strip any remaining illusions from Arianna's sweet eyes.

But that was for the best, right? Even though it felt like a sharpened blade right through his sternum, Arianna deserved better than him. Hadn't he warned her so last night? She hadn't believed him, but she'd believe him now, by God.

And that was enough thinking about and staring at Arianna.

Showtime.

"Hello, family." The smile he tried on for size felt like a wolf's snarl. "Miss me?"

Arianna and Bishop were still gaping, but Arnetta was on the job. "Hello, Joshua," she said, and he had to hand it to the old girl. She said it all calm and breezy-like, as though it'd only been yesterday when he last swam in her pool, sat at her table and watched her television. "How are you?"

"I'm great," he said, because he was. This was what he'd waited for, and he damn sure meant to enjoy it. Sauntering deeper into the room, he put his hands into his pockets and leaned against the mantel, settling beneath that disturbing portrait of Reynolds Warner, the one he'd always hated. "What'd I miss around here while I was gone? Anything?"

His boyhood pals Andrew and Eric had also begun to recover. Unsmiling, they both got up from the sofa and went to stand with the others in a protective gesture that was the rough equivalent of circling the wagons in the face of an Apache attack. They looked serious but not particularly concerned, and Dawson had to tip his invisible hat to them because he knew his sudden appearance had to scare them down to their overpriced loafers.

Andrew, apparently appointing himself family spokesperson for the duration, held out his hand, and they shook. How civilized. "Joshua. What brings you back here?"

Snippets of their shared past rose up to haunt Dawson, and for a minute he had a tough time remembering that they were no longer boys together, running around the grounds looking for deer, snakes or any other creatures they could find, or sneaking into the kitchen to raid the fridge for chicken salad sandwiches and Cook's homemade strawberry ice cream.

"Well, Andrew," he said, "I thought I'd stop by for a minute and let you know what I've been up to for the last several years. Won't that be fun?"

"Joshua." Eric also shook Dawson's hand and then edged closer to Andrew, the two of them forming a united front against Dawson and protecting the others from this unfurling ugliness. "You don't want to do this."

"Actually, I do." Dawson shoved away from the fireplace and helped himself to some coffee from the cart. Taking his time, he sipped appreciatively—man, they always served the best here at Heather Hill, yes siree—before continuing. "Maybe I should start with my name. I changed it, so I'd appreciate it if you'd all stop calling me Joshua. I go by Dawson now. Dawson Reynolds. Nice, huh? It's got a good ring to it."

At this, he couldn't resist a quick glance at Bishop and Arnetta, both of whom gasped. Bishop, whose skin really wasn't looking too good, had something to say about this.

"Your name is Joshua *Bishop.* Don't matter what you change it to. You're the same person you always were."

Dawson checked, his thought process stalling and skidding to a stop.

Surely—surely, God—those words hadn't just come out of that man's mouth. Surely he hadn't said them with a straight face.

You're the same person you always were.

Way to escalate the situation, old man.

Blind fury had Dawson's fist clenched tight enough around the fine china cup to break it. For the first time since he'd arrived this morning, he felt his face heat up and his muscles tighten down, and he worked hard to keep from erupting. The last thing he wanted to do at this long-awaited moment of his life was lose control and let these people know how they'd hurt him.

"Actually, Bishop—"

"Don't call me *Bishop,*" the old man roared.

"—I'm *not* the same person I always was. Prison changed me—"

From the corner of his eye, Dawson saw Arianna's entire body stiffen.

"—and having everyone in my family turn their backs on me also changed me. But I don't want to belabor this whole name thing."

"What the hell do you want, then?" demanded Andrew.

Whoa. Was that an edge he detected in Andrew's voice? Good. With a cool smile, Dawson returned to the sofa, sat, crossed his legs and smoothed the crease in his trousers. And then, because the tension in the room still wasn't quite high enough, he waited for another beat or two before he looked up and met Andrew's killing gaze.

"I came to tell you my great news. Surprise!" Dawson waved his hand with a flourish. "I'm out of prison now."

Absolute silence from all sides.

He'd meant to keep it lighter than this, but Dawson couldn't strip the stone-cold bitterness from his voice. "Of course, that's not really *new* news. I've been out for a while now. Sorry for the delay in getting in touch. I had to spend a little time getting back on my feet, which wasn't easy, let me tell you. I lived in a halfway house for a while, and then I lived with a buddy, then I lived in the buddy's car. Let's see…what else? Oh, yeah. I worked at a car wash, and dug ditches for a landscaper—that was fun—and various other odd jobs so I wouldn't starve to death."

They all stared at him, their eyes round and wide like five sets of dinner platters.

"So while you were getting married and starting a family, Andrew, and you were getting married and starting your family, Eric, I was in counseling trying to deal with my anger-management issues. Apparently I had some problems dealing with prison and then returning to a society that didn't want anything to do with me."

"Jesus." Eric hung his head, running a hand over his face.

"By the way," Dawson said, "I didn't get an invite to either of your weddings. Guess that was a tiny oversight on your parts, huh? Nothing personal against me, right? Well, don't worry. I forgive you."

Andrew and Eric exchanged an indecipherable glance; Arnetta huddled closer to Bishop and Arianna, keeping them in the protective sweep of her arms; Arianna blinked furiously, her eyes sparkling with tears.

Dawson turned his face away from her and continued with his story.

"And then I got a grant from the Phoenix Legacies Foundation. Maybe you've heard of it? Former Virginia governor Beau Taylor runs it. You know Beau, right? Of course you do. He's family. He gave me the funds to start up a house-flipping business, and I made a couple good decisions with investments and whatnot, and now I've got a little money. Not as much as you official Warners have, but still."

He paused, giving someone—anyone—time to react, but they were all still speechless. What? They had nothing to say? No reaction to his long list of hardships and humiliations?

Yeah. No reaction. And he hated them more for it.

His face prickled with growing heat until his ears burned, but he kept his temper on a firm leash, yanking it back like a rabid German shepherd trying to run free and maul everything in its path.

"So, my loving family," he finished, clearing his hoarse throat, "I wanted you to be the first to know—well, not the first, because you all turned your backs on me years ago, but you can be *among* the first—that I didn't rape anyone and I've been completely exonerated of all charges. So you and the rest of the world only *thought* I was a rapist. I *wasn't* a rapist. And I've got the paperwork from the Innocence Program to prove it. Great, huh?"

Bishop held out a placating hand and squeezed between Andrew and Eric, creeping closer like a kid trying to feed a snarling lion a rare steak from his palm.

"Joshua," he said softly, peaceably, "we knew you didn't do it—"

"Bullshit." Dawson took a deep breath, trying to control himself, but a muscle had started ticking in his jaw, and he couldn't get it to stop. "When did you know I didn't do it, I wonder? When you locked the doors against me? When you didn't hire a lawyer for me and let some court-appointed hack represent me? Or was it when you refused to answer my calls from the justice center and prison?"

"Joshua," Bishop tried.

"I'm just trying to understand. Because when you're locked up, you know you have to stand in line to use the phone, right? You know that speaking to someone in the outside world can be your only lifeline, right? But you never took my calls. Was *that* when you had faith in me? Help me out here."

Andrew put a supportive hand on Bishop's shoulder, which pissed Dawson off more than anything else had this morning, because when had anyone ever supported him? When had anyone ever cared that he was hurting or upset?

"You wrote this family off long before you were arrested, Joshua," said Andrew. "You turned your back on us."

"That favor's been returned on all sides, my brother."

"So..." Andrew spoke with slow deliberation, as though he didn't want to disrupt any fragile peace that might break out but also wanted to make sure he understood everyone's relative positions. "We're square, then?"

"Of course," Dawson said.

He shrugged and smiled, trying to look like he didn't understand why such a question was necessary, but no one looked reassured. They all glanced at each other and looked wary and alert, as though they knew another two-ton shoe was about to drop. Dawson would almost laugh, if his gut didn't feel so sick and knotted. That was the thing about life here at Heather Hill: there was always another shoe, another agenda, another lurking betrayal.

People here didn't trust each other, with good reason.

Reaching for a scone, he took a bite, fortifying his strength while he enjoyed the wait. Blueberry. Tasty. Cook hadn't lost any of her skills since he'd been gone, that was for sure. He swallowed, took another big bite and snapped his fingers as though he'd suddenly remembered something.

"There was one other thing," he said out of the side of his mouth.

Everyone stiffened, bracing for the blow.

A muscle now pulsed so prominently in Andrew's jaw and up to his temple that he could barely get the words out. "What's that?"

Dawson licked his fingers and then used a napkin on the residual icing. When that was done, he looked up at Andrew, nailing him right between his eyes with his anger, bitterness and righteous determination.

"I want my birthright and my inheritance. I want my place in the family."

Someone made a low moan at this announcement. Arnetta fished a lacy handkerchief out of the end of her sleeve and dabbled her nose with it. Bishop pressed one hand to his temple and the other to Dawson's arm.

Dawson looked into those wizened brown eyes, kindly now, and felt a twinge of something long buried and forgotten. *Don't fall for this, man,* he told himself, but something was still there between him and Bishop, some connection that wouldn't stay sealed in the past.

Bishop squeezed Dawson's arm with a grip that was strong and sure. And Dawson tried to remember that, before last night, it had been ten years—longer—since he felt this man's touch.

"Joshua." Bishop's voice, gravelly on the best of days, was now froggy with so much emotion it was hard to understand him. "You're my son. That's your birthright. That's the only important thing. You're my son. Mine and Mama's."

That was a low blow, bringing Mama, God rest her beautiful soul, into this mess. Dawson jerked his arm free and wheeled away, shamed because he knew Mama had to be spinning in her grave right now.

"Adopted son," Dawson clarified. "And she wanted me. You never did."

Bishop looked aghast. "That's not true, boy. You know that's not true. I loved you. I treated you like—"

Dawson held up a finger, stopping this self-serving little declaration before it could really get started. "That's the thing, Bishop—"

Bishop erupted, looking for a minute as though he may hit Dawson. "You call me *Daddy,* boy, or so help me—"

"—you didn't treat me like your son." Strangely, Bishop's fury only calmed Dawson down, centered him on this crucial point of his life and the reason he'd turned into the person he now was. "You're not honestly standing there and telling me you treated me the same as you treated, say, *Scooter,* here—" he flapped a hand at Andrew, using Bishop's childhood nickname for him "—or even Eric, are you? Because you didn't. You never did."

"God knows I tried," Bishop said.

"Oh, well, that's different, isn't it? Trying versus doing. You *tried* to teach me to swim, and you *tried* to play checkers with me, and you *tried* to plant tomatoes in the greenhouse with me, but you looked at me different, Bishop. Didn't you? Did you think I didn't notice? Did you think I didn't wonder, from the time I was *five years old,* why my father didn't like me?"

Bishop blinked, but tears rose in his eyes anyway, turning the brown irises into shining crystals. "I did the best I could for you, boy, but—"

Tears? Was this guy for real? He had the nerve to cry these crocodile tears in front of this audience, as though he'd ever given a damn about Dawson? What kind of bullshit was this?

"But I was forced on you. Right, Bishop? You're not going to deny it now, are you? You were happy to throw it in my face the last time we saw each other. Did you all know this?"

He paused here to glance at the others and make sure they felt included in the revelation of this, yet another skeleton from the rattling closets here at Heather Hill. They all stared back at him, silent and riveted.

"Did you all know that's why we fell out? Because saintly Bishop here got fed up with me and my partying ways and my drinking, and decided to tell me I was no son of his. Did you know this? Huh? And he was none too gentle about this news, let me tell you. He took the opportunity to tell me how he'd never wanted me and would never have taken me, and I gotta tell you, it hurt a little. Didn't do much for my self-esteem."

The sarcasm was a defensive measure, and he clung to it. These people could never know how that one scene, that one fight with his so-called father, had hurt him and altered the course of his life. No one could ever know how that one conversation had ruined him, probably forever. He could never reveal how that one moment had sent him on the trajectory that ended in a wrongful accusation and prison.

Bishop hung his head and lost it for a minute, his shoulders shaking with quiet sobs. The rest of them watched with concern, hovering, not sure whether touching him would make him cry harder or not, but Dawson watched the display, unmoved. And when Bishop looked up with his tear-slicked face, Dawson's iron heart didn't so much as twitch.

"I'm sorry," Bishop said. "You have to forgive this old man, son. I'm so—"

Sorry. Well, didn't that just beat all?

"I'm not really in a forgiving mood today, Bishop, so we'll have to put that on the shelf for now. What I really want to talk about—"

"Joshua," Andrew said, a distinct note of warning in his voice.

Dawson ignored him. "—is my real father. My birth father."

Andrew shot a worried glance at Arnetta. "Now is not the time—"

Dawson waved a dismissive hand. "Oh, don't worry about her. She knows who my real father is. Don't you, Arnetta?"

A ripple of shock traveled around the room. Arianna and Eric, he was guessing, were shocked because they didn't know this bit of family history. Bishop, Arnetta and Andrew, on the other hand, were no doubt shocked only because he'd decided to say it aloud, like this.

But then Arnetta surprised him. Dabbing at her shining eyes, she straightened, replaced the handkerchief up her sleeve and squared her shoulders. "Yes."

"What the hell is going on here?" Eric demanded, but he was apparently already putting two and two together, because his gaze flickered up over the mantel to the portrait of the glowering man, who had never, as far as anyone knew, kept his shit in his pants and had therefore probably fathered enough bastards to populate a small town.

"Arnetta knows," Dawson said quietly, glad to get to this central truth about his life at long last, "that her dead husband, the late, great Reynolds Warner, got one of the maids pregnant—there's probably more than one, but we'll stick to one for now, at least until any other bastards step forward to claim their rights—and she had a baby. Me. And when a car hit that poor maid while she was waiting at the bus stop when I was a year old, Reynolds Warner foisted me on Bishop and his wife. Isn't that right?"

"Yes," Arnetta said.

"Oh, my God," Arianna breathed. She pressed a hand to her heart. *"Oh, my God."*

Andrew and Eric exchanged darkly significant looks—they were probably running mental calculations, trying to figure out how their inheritances had just shrunk with the appearance of a new heir—and Arnetta and Bishop clasped hands, apparently giving each other strength.

How touching.

"What do you want, Joshua?" Bishop stood tall, his voice unwavering. Maybe he was getting used to the idea that Dawson wasn't going to disappear into the woodwork again for another ten years. "How can we make this right?"

Dawson stared at him. Did he really think anything was that easy? "I don't want anything from you, old man, and you can't make anything right—"

Bishop flinched.

"—but I do want a paternity test to get my parentage straightened out just, you know, for the record, and then I want my rightful share of WarnerBrands International and the family's other holdings." He paused. "Any questions? Yes? No?"

All the air seemed to have gone out of the room, leaving everyone incapable of speech. Dawson felt immensely satisfied on the one hand and oddly deflated on the other, and the ambivalence made his head spin. He wanted this. He'd earned it. He was only asking for what was rightfully his—a place in the family, with all its accoutrements—and he would not feel guilty for it. They owed him, and there was no shame in claiming what belonged to him.

So, no. He would not feel bad. Nothing and no one would ruin this moment for him. Not even Arianna, whose steady, reproachful gaze on his face this whole time felt like two glowing-hot fireplace pokers piercing his flesh down to the bone.

"Nothing?" He waited, but no one spoke. "Well, I guess that's it, then."

He put his coffee cup back on the cart with a clink and used a napkin to wipe his hands, which were, he was dismayed to realize, experiencing a slight tremble.

Savoring the room's absolute silence—only the Tomb of the Unknowns in the dead of night was more hushed than this—he tossed the napkin aside and strode for the door. Halfway there, though, he couldn't resist one last verbal jab, which he tossed over his shoulder.

"I enjoyed catching up with you all. We really should do it more often."

Chapter 6

Dawson walked out, his steps quicker than they needed to be. Not because he was running away or any punk-ass thing like that—just because it was time to make his exit before someone else tried to grab the last word. And his face and palms weren't hot and sweaty from nerves—it was adrenaline and triumph that had him so hopped up right now. Nothing else. And the look on his father's—no, Bishop's—face, all that hurt and anguish, the sorrow and the guilt, meant nothing to him now. It was far too little, way too late.

He made it down the long hallway and through the massive foyer. Past the curving staircase and out the front door, his face grotesquely distorted by the cut glass on either side.

Taking the shallow steps one at a time, he crunched onto the gravel drive and headed for his rental. The car was his only focus. It seemed like a lush tropical oasis in the midst of a category 5 hurricane, and he was desperate to get there.

Only, he couldn't seem to breathe, and he couldn't work up that victorious feeling he'd anticipated. All he felt was the same old echoing hollowness deep inside him, and—this was a big surprise—bewilderment. Because he still couldn't, even now, figure out how he and the people who'd once meant everything in the world to him had come to face off on opposite sides of this scorched battlefield.

He'd just reached for the door handle with one hand and dug into his pocket for his keys with the other, when he heard her. Actually, he felt her first, that subtle shifting of awareness that announced her like Ed McMahon announcing Johnny Carson.

He glanced around in time to see the front door bang open and Arianna storm out, just over five feet of furious vengeance ready to drop-kick him into next week even though she had to weigh half what he did.

Ah, man. That disdain in her eyes hurt. Sucker punched him in the forehead with enough force to drop him to his knees. They stared at each other, the tension stretching and coiling them into a stranglehold, until it suddenly felt crucial to reject her before she rejected him the way everyone else in his life had rejected him.

Unfortunately, she drew first blood before he could get his mouth working.

"Are you proud of yourself?"

Well, there it was: her inevitable disappointment and bitter disillusionment with him. It was almost a relief to get them out of the way, although he missed last night's glowing warmth in her expression. But at least now she knew who and what he was, and he didn't have to pretend to be a worthwhile human being.

Having perfected his indifferent act back in the cradle,

it wasn't too hard to smile and shrug. "I told you that you could do better than me."

"This isn't about you and me." Her hands fisted at her sides. "There is no you and me."

No, there wasn't, but he didn't like hearing her say it.

Diverted, just like that, he put the family drama on the back burner and focused on her. What they'd done last night. What they'd been to each other, what he'd touched and tasted, what they'd said. The memories made his blood sizzle, and he didn't bother trying to keep it out of his gaze as it skated over her incredible body, which was hidden beneath summer cotton and flowers now, but never forgotten.

"Is that right?" he murmured.

"Yes." Her chin hitched higher with open defiance, but she couldn't hide the way her cheeks brightened with a flush. "You took care of that when you disappeared."

"I'm sorry." Had he ever produced a lamer understatement? *Sorry* was for forgetting to pick up milk on your way home. *Sorry* didn't cover hurting Arianna's feelings after she'd given herself to him with such amazing abandon, or the gut-deep sickness he felt at having missed the opportunity to spend more time with her. "I ran into Bishop after you went inside, and I—"

"Had to duck and run like a coward?"

This appraisal, unfortunately, hit way too close to home. "Decided to leave before the situation escalated."

"That's funny. You weren't too concerned about escalation just now."

"Just now I said a few things that were years in the making, and I said them on my terms."

"And as hurtfully as possible. Congratulations. You must be thrilled."

He felt his mouth twist. "They had it coming."

"Really?"

"Really."

"Well, great. So they hurt you and you hurt them and everything's even. The question now is: What're you going to do about it?"

"Weren't you paying attention? I just did what I'm going to do about it. I want my fair share. I asked them to give it to me. If they don't, I'll take it."

She paused, her eyes glinting with amusement. "You don't really believe that, do you?"

"Pardon me?"

"This isn't about your fair share, only you're too blind to see it. This is about you wanting to belong somewhere. This is about you wanting to belong *here*." She waved a hand at the mansion, but he couldn't look anywhere but at her, especially when her face softened with an expression that looked like understanding. "This is about your hurt."

He turned away, some unidentifiable emotion making his mouth dry and his tongue thick. *Hurt.*

Was that the word you used when the man you'd thought was your father disclaimed you because he'd never really loved or wanted you and didn't approve of your hard-drinking, hard-partying lifestyle? When the people you'd grown up with believed you were capable of violence against women, and turned their faces away when you were accused of heinous acts? When you yourself were so stubborn and unforgiving that you preferred to take your chances with a public defender rather than ask said so-called family for help? When you had faith in both the justice system and your college buddy, the one who really committed the crime, expecting them to do the right thing by you, and they let you down in the worst possible way?

When no one in your life was who they seemed to be, and they all seemed to be taking numbers and standing in line, waiting for their chance to stab you in the heart with betrayal?

Hurt. Yeah. That was one word for it.

"I'm not hurt," he lied, sidling closer and enjoying the corresponding flash of alarm in her glittering eyes. Lust flared, collecting in his tight throat and making his voice hoarse. "And you're showing a lot of interest in someone you've written off, little girl."

Some demon possessed him, an undeniable force he couldn't resist. And since she wasn't moving away fast enough, Dawson didn't even try to resist. Reaching out, he stroked his thumb across her bottom lip, which was plump and dewy-soft, like one of Arnetta's precious roses after a summer shower. Arianna submitted, her breath spiking. He was just about to press his luck and possibly risk his life by seeing what else she'd allow, when she caught herself and smacked his hand away.

"Don't touch me. And don't change the subject."

He froze, both his hand and his spirit stung by this rebuke. Being denied the right to touch her, after last night's orgy of feeling, taste and smell, was unnatural, and he felt the outrage he imagined a hungry baby would feel when denied his mother's breast.

She was tying him in knots, this girl. On every level, from his emotions to his seething and overloaded hormonal response to her, she'd turned him out.

This, naturally, made him crazy. And when he was crazy, he lashed out.

"You didn't mind me touching you last night."

Her face went the DayGlo red of a stoplight, and her choked fury was so strong it almost silenced her. "Don't you dare throw that in my face."

"I don't want to throw it in your face." He shrugged, shifting closer until there wasn't space enough for even a ray of the morning's light to shine between them. "I just want to repeat it."

To her credit, Arianna stood her ground as he loomed over her, refusing to budge. He liked that about her; he hated that about her.

"There won't be any repeats."

His outrage inched higher, approaching a danger zone. "Now that you know I'm an ex-con?"

"Now that I know you're a bitter SOB who doesn't care how much he hurts his elderly father."

Dawson stilled, his head on the verge of explosion. "I don't have a father. All I have is the man who did a half-assed job raising me."

He turned toward the car, with Arianna right in his face. "Dawson." He kept going because this was getting old and he couldn't stand another minute of her hating him, but she didn't give up. "Wait."

"I'm out." He opened the door and stuck his right foot inside, ready to drive all the way to Anchorage if that's what he needed to do to get away from here, away from her.

But then she played dirty, putting her soft little hand on top of his where it rested on the door. "Please."

Helpless to do otherwise, he waited, cursing himself for a punk and a fool.

"Bishop loves you." Arianna squeezed his fingers. "I know he does. It doesn't have to be this way. You can rebuild your relationship with—"

He shook his head but couldn't bear to pull his hand away and break the contact between them. "Ah, now, see, you almost had me, but then you had to push it. There's nothing there to rebuild. Never was."

"Bishop is old, Dawson. How much longer do you think the two of you have to fix your relationship? I know he has regrets. And I know you well enough to know you'll regret it if you leave things like this between you."

This was another of her eerie views into the deepest corner of his soul, and man, it was like nails across a chalkboard. In stereo. Risking it at last, he stared her in the face, infusing his gaze with ice and doing his best to scare her shitless so she'd back away and drop this topic forever.

"You don't know a damn thing about me, sweet Ari."

And that little girl, that tiny little woman with more balls than the running bulls of Pamplona and the wisdom of a Tibetan monk, looked at him with clear eyes, spoke in a quiet voice and knocked the wind right out of him.

"I know you're not a rapist. I never would have believed that about you for one second."

The words went through him like a lightning strike, because here, finally, was the one thing he'd longed to hear more than anything else.

Christ.

He wanted to leave, but more than that, he wanted someone to know, understand and forgive him for that thing he'd never even done. "My buddy and I," he began urgently, with no idea where this confession was coming from, "we went to a bar."

"You don't have to—"

"There was a woman. She flirted with me. I would have gone home with her, but I wasn't that into her and didn't want to deal with the hassle. So I left. He stayed."

She waited, braced for the worst in every motionless part of her body.

Now that he'd gotten this far into the story, it was harder to finish than he'd thought. Way harder. He swallowed, trying to scrape some of the bitterness out of his throat. "He…slipped her something. A date-rape drug. He had fun. She didn't. In the morning, it was my face she remembered." Another swallow. "Not his."

"Oh, God—"

"When the police came calling, my good buddy, who used a condom so there'd be no evidence, clammed up. Big surprise, huh? And she was a convincing witness. So I went to jail. Did not pass Go, did not collect $200. The end."

"But how did you—"

"Get out? After years of therapy and working through it in her mind, she realized I wasn't the one. Then she worked with the Innocence Program and got me out. Thank God."

There it was: the worst. The ugliest things that had ever been said—or believed—about him. The allegations weren't true, but that'd never stopped anyone from turning away from him and writing him off.

Arianna was probably like all the rest.

Except…

God, he hoped she wasn't like all the rest.

Staring at the ground now because he couldn't meet her eyes while she made her judgment, he waited.

To his utter astonishment, she reached up and stroked his throbbing jaw with her soft fingers. When he worked up the courage to look, he saw the sparkle of tears in her eyes and had to remind himself that it wouldn't be too cool to drop to his knees and kiss her feet with gratitude.

"I'm sorry you went through that," she said simply. "You didn't deserve it."

That put him right over the edge.

Undone, he got into the car and drove away, spewing gravel in his wake.

* * *

Arianna hurried back inside, to the unfolding chaos in the library.

Everyone had retreated to separate corners of the room, from whence they snarled at each other. Eric was at the bar, mixing up what appeared to be a gallon-sized pitcher of Bloody Marys. Andrew prowled back and forth in front of the French doors, relentless as a caged panther with a nail in his paw. Huddled in the corner, whispering urgently together, stood Aunt Arnetta and Bishop. None of them looked around when she walked in.

Eric added several dashes of hot sauce to the pitcher and spoke over his shoulder to no one in particular. "It seems like a pertinent question."

"Well, it's not." Andrew reached a dead end at the far wall, pivoted and came back, shoving his fists deep into his trousers.

"I'm just wondering how many more of Grandfather's kids are going to come out of the woodwork." With the pitcher finally mixed to his satisfaction, Eric filled a tumbler almost to the top, turned to the glowering portrait over the fireplace, raised his glass in a toast and took a healthy swallow. "Has anyone got any idea how many separate baby mamas we're dealing with?"

Andrew, shooting a glance at Aunt Arnetta, issued a warning. "Eric—"

"Just give me a round number that I can work with." Eric drank again, smacking his lips and being as obnoxious as possible. "Ten? Thirty? Fifty—"

"Oh, for God's sake," Aunt Arnetta muttered, exchanging a dark glance with Bishop.

"—Or is it a cyclical thing? We can expect a new Warner to pop up every third year? Or during election years? Or does it have to do with when they hold the winter

Olympics?" Eric held his hands wide in a beseeching gesture. "Someone help me out here."

Andrew stopped pacing to stare at Eric with the full might of his displeasure. "Eric? Now would be the perfect time for you to shut the hell up. Okay? Arnetta doesn't need this right now. Neither does Bishop."

Eric gave a sharp nod and grabbed the pitcher for a refill. "Fair enough."

"Thank you." Andrew went back to the French doors and stared out at the pool.

Aunt Arnetta and Bishop, taking advantage of the momentary lull, sat on the nearest sofa. Arianna crept a little farther into the room, wondering what her role here was.

"And why am I always the last one to know?" His glass full again, Eric wheeled around to demand more answers. "Why does everyone in this family know about all the skeletons in that man's closet—" he jerked a thumb over his shoulder at the portrait "—but me? It's like he's got an elephant graveyard in there or something. Seriously. How many mistresses did he—"

Aunt Arnetta surged to her feet, all gentility gone. *"Eric."*

Eric, perhaps sensing doom, froze, his mouth hanging open.

"Shut. Up." Aunt Arnetta glared at him, making Andrew's fearsome glower of a moment ago look like a smile from Santa Claus.

They all gaped, probably because no one in living memory had ever seen Arnetta Warner be anything other than the perfect lady. This, clearly, was a bad sign.

Eric recovered first. "S-sorry, Grandmother."

Aunt Arnetta, giving him a satisfied nod, resumed her

seat and crossed her legs. "Thank you. May I have a drink, please? Make it a double vodka."

Arianna, shaking off the lingering shock effects of this outburst, snuck a glance at the pendulum's slow swing on the grandfather clock in the corner. Ten-twenty. At this rate, they'd all be staggering by noon.

Ah, well. When in Rome...

"And I'll have a Bloody Mary," she told Eric.

Eric raised his eyebrows. "Are you even legal?"

Arianna didn't have the time or patience for nonsense. "Don't make me come over there."

Muttering unintelligibly, Eric reached for another tumbler.

Drinks were made and passed around. Arianna sat on a love seat and tasted her Bloody Mary, which was spicy enough to keep her sinuses clear for weeks to come. Andrew and Eric sat as well. They all stared at each other, sipping and brooding. No one spoke.

Dawson Reynolds crept into the silence, owning her thoughts as he had since she laid eyes on him. No. Not Dawson Reynolds. Joshua Bishop. She'd have to work on remembering that.

Was it just last night that she met him? Was that possible? What did she think about before he showed up in her life? Anything?

So...just to review: Last night, she'd met and fallen wildly in lust with a man she thought was named Dawson Reynolds. They flirted, they had sex in the greenhouse, he disappeared, she cried.

Today, it turned out that Dawson Reynolds was an innocent ex-convict named Joshua Bishop, who was the adopted son of Franklin Bishop, her aunt's right-hand man, and the biological son of Arianna's late and apparently unlamented Uncle Reynolds. Dawson/Joshua hated the

Warners, and they weren't any too fond of him. He wanted his share of the pie, and they no doubt wanted to be left alone to continue their unbroken streak of dominance in the corporate world.

To summarize, then: pretty much everyone here at Heather Hill had a deep secret and/or wasn't what s/he seemed to be and/or had betrayed or been betrayed by another family member.

Nice, huh?

Maybe Microsoft or Google could design software sophisticated enough to track all these hidden relationships; it really was hard to keep up.

The best part of all was that Arianna also had a secret. Well, she had more than one, seeing as how she'd dodged some of Dawson's questions last night, but that wasn't the one on her mind now.

No. The troublesome secret for the moment was this: A remote, shameful part of her was glad to see Dawson/ Joshua/Whoever again. Glad to know who he was and where he came from. Glad to know she could find him again if she needed to. Glad to see that he hadn't forgotten their interlude last night and wasn't immune to her this morning.

Yeah. They all had serious mental-health issues here at Heather Hill, didn't they? Must be something in the water.

Another sip of her powerful Bloody Mary had a buzz shooting straight to her brain, which was good because her brain could use a little relief from its overload. On the other hand, it was bad because how could she think clearly about a complex problem like Dawson when she was already half a sheet to the wind?

She got him now, though. Totally understood the wounded eyes and the mountain-sized chip on his shoulder.

There wasn't a man alive who wouldn't be enraged over the loss of years of his life for no good reason. And to have also lost the love of his family, and not even have them to rely on in his time of need, well…

She couldn't imagine the damage that must have been done to Dawson.

Joshua.

Whoever.

Suddenly, nonsensically, she was mad, too, and the hurt Dawson had caused by walking out on her last night seemed like a big, fat nothing. She was tough; she'd get over it. She'd punish him for it, of course, but she would get over it.

But what about Dawson? Would he ever get over the hurts he'd suffered at the hands of his family?

What kind of so-called father rejected his son, adopted or not?

Turning to Bishop, she studied him. They'd become friendly during her visit, and if anyone had asked her two hours ago, she'd've said he was a fine gentleman, the kind they didn't make anymore.

Now, though, she saw him as an old man who'd royally screwed up the most important task he—or anyone—could have in life: raising his child.

Andrew, meanwhile, sighed and ran a hand through his hair, ruffling it. Like the others, he seemed to have aged ten years this morning, and the stress lines showed on his face. "There are a couple ways we could go with this," he began. "We could fight him, of course, and force his hand on the—"

"I don't understand this, Bishop." Arianna spoke quietly, but there was no keeping the ferocity out of her voice. Who in this crowd would speak up for Dawson if she didn't? "What did you do to him?"

They all gaped at her, except for Bishop. He sat, shell-shocked and frozen, on the edge of the sofa, his hands on his knees and his gaze on the floor.

He didn't answer and seemed not to breathe. His coloring was definitely off now, chalky, and his face was damp with what looked like a clammy sweat.

"Arianna," Aunt Arnetta said, "this is none of your concern."

Arianna considered this, her gaze still on Bishop. "True. But I'm trying to understand. I can't figure out how this man I thought I knew a little bit, this fine gentleman, could have turned his back on his son. How he could have thrown his paternity in his face. Have I misjudged you that badly, Bishop?"

Bishop stirred for the first time, staring off at something just beyond the coffee table, a memory that only he could see. "Joshua was a hard boy. You can't understand that now, but he was. Hardheaded. Never listened. Always made his own path." He paused just long enough to let the beginnings of a smile flicker across his face. "And he was *smart*. Way smarter than me, and I never finished high school." His faint smile vanished. "I couldn't handle him."

So what? What did this have to do with disowning Dawson and letting him molder in jail for something he didn't do? "I still don't—"

The harshness in her voice seemed to snap Bishop out of the past and put him firmly in the here and now. His lips twisted with a wry grin. "You're awful hard on me, Arianna. How many children you got?"

Was that supposed to shut her up? "You'll have to do better than that, Bishop. You can deflect all you want, but that doesn't change what you did."

"Arianna," Aunt Arnetta snarled.

Bishop held up a hand. "Let the girl speak, Arnetta. She's right. Well…half-right, anyway. That boy went off to Duke. Started drinking. Running with the wrong crowd. Got into all kinds of trouble, and I let him know. I didn't want no son of mine acting like an ass down there."

"So?" Arianna said. "That's the story of half the kids in this country."

Bishop blinked at her, his gaze hardening. "He cussed me. Said I was nothing but a butler who spent his whole life waiting on folk, being a second-class citizen, and what did I know? He said he wished he had a daddy he could be proud of, like one of the Warner men up at the big house—"

"Oh, Bishop." Aunt Arnetta put a consoling arm around his shoulders.

"—and he didn't never…didn't never want to wind up like me."

The effort of getting this last part out seemed to take a real toll. Bishop raised a gnarled hand to his temple and rubbed, as though he needed to soothe away an unreachable pain. That hand shook and his lower lip trembled. Hurt pride practically leaked from him, and he was such a perfect mirror for his son's wounded teddy bear soul that Arianna couldn't look away.

Neither could anyone else, apparently. All eyes were riveted on Bishop.

"He stabbed me in the heart, that boy." Bishop looked to each face in turn, seeking understanding, desperate for absolution. Andrew nodded at him, but Eric lowered his gaze, looking intensely uncomfortable. Aunt Arnetta rubbed his back. "Stabbed me *right in my heart.*"

Arianna didn't so much as blink. How could she grant forgiveness when she wasn't done accusing? This ugliness between parent and child was unimaginable to her. She thought of Daddy, God rest his soul, and Mother, home in NYC, with a box of Godiva's hazelnut praline truffles always at the ready, just in case Arianna decided to pop home for the weekend. Even when she'd driven her parents crazy, and there'd been plenty of that over the years, there wasn't one second of her life when she'd doubted their love for her, or her place in the family.

Dawson, on the other hand, had grown up in a house where he wasn't quite loved and didn't quite belong. And they'd wondered why he had anger issues?

"So you stabbed him back," she said to Bishop. "You told him he wasn't yours."

To his credit, Bishop didn't try to minimize the ugliness. "Worst mistake of my life. Biggest regret I've ever had. I broke that boy's heart, and my wife's heart, and she never got over it. Broke my own heart." He paused. "I never got over it."

Andrew stared off across the room, looking thoughtful. "That must've been when Joshua really spiraled out of control. Right after he graduated. He had a couple DUIs and a drunk-and-disorderly. We bailed him out the first couple of times. It only pissed him off. He didn't want anything from a Warner. He told me to go screw myself."

Bishop nodded. "That boy was trying to destroy himself. I knew what he was doing. I couldn't stop it. And when he was arrested for sexual assault, I tried—"

"You didn't try hard enough," Arianna said flatly.

There was a general hiss of disapproval around the group, and to her dismay, Andrew's gaze sharpened on her with the keen intensity of a hawk. "What's all this to you, Ari?" he questioned. "You weren't here then. You don't know anything about this. Why are you Joshua's biggest defender all of a sudden? I didn't think you two even knew each other."

Arianna froze, suddenly feeling as conspicuous as a flying hippopotamus.

Damn it. When would she learn to keep her big mouth shut?

"It don't matter." With a choked, broken sound, Bishop curled in on himself, wrapping his arms around his abdomen and rocking back and forth where he sat. "She's right. I wasn't ever the father that boy needed."

This, finally, cracked the buildup of ice around her heart. It was such a stunning and horrifying thing to see Bishop lose control—*Bishop!* who'd run this household and successfully navigated the stormy waters of Aunt Arnetta's moods since Adam and Eve put on their first set of clothes—that Arianna wanted to hang her head in shame for everything she'd just said to him.

Poor man. Look at him. He knew what he'd done, and all the ways he'd failed.

"I'm sorry, Bishop," Arianna began.

Aunt Arnetta had already moved into damage-control mode. "You hush now, Bishop." Pulling out that same lace hanky, she tried to press it into his hand so he could wipe his streaming eyes, but Bishop's fingers were shaking so badly he only dropped it. "Everything'll be okay. You stop that crying."

Bishop, to their intense embarrassment, didn't stop crying. Worse, he seemed to have passed into some other realm where he had to plead his case and no amount of reassurance could reach him.

"Joshua," he said, sobbing and rocking, his voice garbled with emotion and drool trickling from the corner of his mouth, "please sorry can't me not blame." One half of his face spasmed, and unwrapping his hands from his body, he pressed them to the sides of his head. "Blame not Joshua sorry Joshaaa. *Joshaaa.*"

"Hush, Bishop," Aunt Arnetta said, still trying to soothe him.

Arianna, Andrew and Eric, meanwhile, exchanged looks of alarm. This wasn't normal, was it? Something else was going on here, because a man shouldn't—

"Bishop," Arianna cried, reaching out to him. "Are you okay?"

They watched in stunned disbelief as Bishop's eyes rolled back in his head. Before anyone could stop him, he slumped over sideways, his dead weight knocking Aunt Arnetta down with him.

"Bishop!" Arnetta screamed.

"Somebody call 911," Andrew said grimly.

Chapter 7

A couple hours later, Arianna pounded on Dawson's door with her palm and, fueled by frustration, raised her voice. "I need to talk to you. *Dawson.*"

She shot a quick glance over her shoulder down the long, plush hallway. Empty, thank God. Five-star hotels like this generally didn't take kindly to people banging on the guests' doors, but she had more important things to worry about than being arrested for disturbing the peace.

Hearing no movement inside, she knocked again.

"Damn it, Dawson, I know you're in there, and I don't appreciate—"

Without warning, the door swung open, and there Dawson was, cell phone in hand, naked but for the white towel across his hips and the drops of water sprinkling his skin.

Oh, man.

Despite the crisis, her hormones were fully functional. Overactive, in fact. She wanted to scoop him up and devour him, one delicious bite at a time, like a DQ Oreo Blizzard. She wanted him between her legs again, inside her, their sweat mingling in an intoxicating musk. She wanted to lock herself inside that room with him and never come out.

All of which proved, once again, that she had the IQ of a newborn hamster where this man was concerned.

They stared at each other in mutual speechlessness until finally her face burned so red-hot with embarrassment that she had to lower her gaze and pray for composure.

She hadn't expected this. Well, she'd expected him to answer the door, obviously, because this was his hotel room. But she hadn't expected him to look like…*that.*

You'd think that a near-naked Dawson wouldn't hit her so hard, having had sex with him last night and all, but no. Last night, she hadn't seen all *this.* And all *this* was magnificent.

Acres of dewy bare skin, gleaming warm and brown in the early afternoon light. Shoulders and arms cut with muscles so defined they probably required a *Rocky*-style championship bout workout, with one-arm push-ups and whatnot, to achieve. That unidentifiable tattoo on his neck, which she now saw was a grid like a tic-tac-toe board, with swirls at the ends. A rippling abdomen. Strong thighs, heavy calves, nice feet. Even in her flustered foolishness, she didn't dare peek at the towel and what it hid, but man, she wanted to.

Feeling strangled, she cleared her throat.

"Arianna?"

That raw huskiness in his voice snapped her out of her sensual reverie.

What was she doing? This wasn't about admiring the

jerk's badass body, or remembering delicious snippets of last night. This was an emergency.

"I need to talk to you." Shoring up her courage, she looked back in his face and wished she hadn't. There was such heat in those dark eyes, such flashing desire, that she knew something had to be going on underneath that towel.

Another excruciating second passed.

Em-er-gen-cy.

Shouldering past him and into his room, she ignored the electric contact of their arms and glanced around. It was a suite, with tasteful modern sofas and tables, potted plants and a bar area, and enough space for a family of four to live comfortably until the kids went off to college. She'd expected as much. Dawson, having come into his money fairly recently, apparently liked to roll with style, and she couldn't blame him for that.

"Come right in." He shut the door behind her.

"Where have you been? We've been calling and calling you."

His expression turned wary. "I…was blowing off some steam in the hotel's weight room. What's up?"

"I left you a thousand messages." All the morning's mounting frustrations rose up to make her a little manic. "I had to call your office and sweet talk your assistant into telling me your cell phone number and what hotel you were at. And then I had to bribe the front desk clerk to tell me your room number. Why didn't you check your messages?"

"I just was." He held up the cell phone. "What's going on?"

Now that her desperate find-Dawson mission was accomplished and the moment was here, she couldn't say it. She hated to hurt this man any further. The frustration on top of the worry, naturally, made her snippy.

"I don't even know what to call you," she said sourly.

After a long hesitation, he shrugged with what looked like real confusion. As though the whole topic was as big a mystery to him as it was to her.

"I don't know what you should call me, either."

Great.

"I have some bad news for you..."

He stilled.

"Bishop collapsed after you left. He's in critical condition at the hospital. They're running tests, but...we think he's had a stroke."

"Oh."

She waited, but that was all he said. Just *oh*.

She was beginning to reflect on the general heartlessness of both father and son in the misbegotten Bishop family when she saw it: a subtle contraction of all his features, with a look of such fleeting but abject pain that she almost missed it.

Then—oh, no—then he blindly reached behind him, found the coffee table and sank onto it. Putting his elbows on his knees, he clasped his hands together and rested his forehead against his fists, either praying desperately or trying to pull himself back from the brink of despair.

Oh, God. What did she do now?

She crept closer, her hands itching to touch him and provide some comfort, but her mangled pride kept her on a short leash. So she hovered, trying to be the voice of calm in his crisis.

"So we need to get to the hospital."

He nodded.

"I'll drive you."

He nodded again.

"You should get dress—"

Suddenly he looked up at her, his eyes dry but way too bright, almost feral. "He'll be okay, won't he?"

It would have been so nice to lie, but she couldn't do that. If nothing else, he deserved the truth. "I don't know," she said helplessly.

A third nod, and then his face twisted and he rested his forehead against his hands again. His shoulders heaved, and that was more than she could take. Whether he was a jerk or not—and they would get to the bottom of that issue sooner or later—he needed her now. And as she'd already discovered last night, she couldn't turn away from this man.

She put a hand on his nape, caressing the soft, damp thatch of dreadlocks and trying to soothe him, just a little. He looked up again, but now he didn't seem so lost in his pain. He studied her, his gaze searching her face for unknowable things. And then he tried to smile.

"Most holy, huh?"

That got her. She almost laughed. "I'm a regular angel."

"I know," he said, serious now, and then he pulled her to him.

Pressing his cheek to her breasts, he held her and she held him back, and she forgot, or maybe decided not to remember, that she'd spent most of last night hating his guts and swearing that she'd never let him, or any other man, get to her again.

"Thank you, angel," he whispered.

"You're welcome," she said, pulling him closer.

Arianna navigated the endless maze of colored tape on the floor, turning right here and left there, leading them into the depths of the building that could very well be the place where his father died. Dawson trailed after her, feeling lost and also somehow found, and he couldn't shake the unaccountable certainty that things could only be so bad if Arianna was with him. After an elevator ride, they arrived outside a section of the hospital with an ominous overhead sign: Neuro-ICU.

He checked at the juncture of the nurses' station and the waiting area, his feet incapable of taking him through those double doors.

Jesus, Pop. I don't want it to end like this.

"I found him," Arianna announced.

She veered into a large private room just off the main waiting area, with Dawson on her heels. The small, tasteful sign to this private enclave, he noted with disgust, identified it as the Reynolds Warner Lounge. Typical. His so-called family threw their money around and ruled whichever tiny corner of the world they could reach.

The generalized surliness that was as much a part of his genetic makeup as his height and bone structure kicked in, and he hovered in the doorway, frozen with an indecision that only grew when he saw the avid faces all around the room. Wasn't this just a cozy little extension of the scene in the library this morning? Sofas and chairs; scowls and coffee. The only things that'd changed were the locale and the paper cups that substituted for Arnetta's fine china.

Like magic, every expression darkened when they saw him, every mouth thinned. He told himself it didn't matter—would never matter—but it did.

Well…screw them.

Backing up a step, he addressed Arianna, the only one worth a damn out of the whole bunch. "I'll just wait out here—"

Imperious Andrew, sitting on a chair in the corner by the window, looking like some third-world despot posing for a statue, snorted. "What's the matter, Joshua? I thought you were so anxious to claim your rightful place. Why not stay in the Warner lounge with the Warners? Afraid we might have some words for you—"

"Andrew," Arianna snarled.

"—or that someone might point out that this is your fault?"

Heat shot up Dawson's face, a blast of scorching orange lava from some emotional volcano deep inside him. Andrew was right, of course, and they all knew it. This was Dawson's fault, and his malignant spite was to blame for the old man lying in the hospital bed down the hall. And if Bishop died—

No. He wouldn't go there.

He wouldn't be shamed. Not here, not by Andrew. He'd survived things in prison that would make a lesser man, like Andrew, scuttle under the table and curl into the fetal position, and he'd survive the awkwardness of this moment, where the truth was the worst possible weapon against him.

Leveling his hardest gaze at his half brother—*You want a piece of me, man? Well, bring it*—he strode all the way into the room and brought the subject around to the only thing that mattered right now.

"How is he, Arnetta?"

Poor Arnetta was so shell-shocked and grave, her color so translucently pale, her eyes so wide with bewilderment, that she didn't answer. Her silver-fox bob was ruffled, as though she'd been running her hands through it, and she seemed beyond tears or emotion, beyond anything but staunch terror. She sat alone on a love seat, her rigid spine not touching the back, and the place beside her, where Bishop would normally sit, was empty.

"Arnetta?" he repeated softly.

Arianna was already in motion. Sweeping past Dawson with a flutter of her skirt and the fleeting scent of flowers, she took Arnetta's hand and settled beside her. This roused Arnetta enough to blink and look around at Arianna, to flash her the quick beginnings of a reassuring smile.

Eric, meanwhile, took mercy on Dawson, though he didn't look particularly happy about it. "The surgeon was in right before you came. He's had a transient ischemic attack—a TIA."

"A mini stroke?" Dawson wasn't sure whether this was good news or bad.

"Basically," Eric agreed. "He's got major blockages in his carotid arteries. They're prepping him for surgery."

Holy shit. "What—*now?*"

This seemed to be more than Andrew could take. Uncurling from his chair, he walked toward Dawson and didn't stop until he was right in his face. "Yeah, *now.* That seemed like the best option, seeing as how they're trying to save his life." He sneered. "Not that you care one way or the other."

The low-level buzzing Dawson had been hearing reached a crescendo and burst open, as though a hornet's nest had exploded inside his head. Without thought, he lunged for Andrew's throat and the two of them clashed with the force of charging sumo wrestlers. "No," cried one of the women, but Dawson was impervious to everything but the need to reach down Andrew's throat and pull his tongue out by the roots.

They struggled together, ricocheting off one wall and hitting another, Eric trying to come between them and giving it a good effort, the women hovering. Dawson saw nothing but the rage-distorted face of the man he'd grown up with and loved like a brother. The man who'd turned his back on him years ago and blamed him now. The man whose betrayal had hurt the worst next to Bishop's.

The man whose features he was going to rearrange into mincemeat.

Jerking one arm free and balling his fist, ready to launch Andrew into next month, Dawson hit something with his elbow. Arianna yelped.

That one moment of clarity cut through Dawson's rage and left a stark terror that made the news of Bishop's collapse seem like a Candygram.

Not Arianna, God.

Wheeling around, he discovered her in a sprawled heap on the floor, rubbing her shoulder and grimacing. Dawson hit the floor beside her, propelled by some combination of his knees giving way and the raw, desperate need to make sure he hadn't hurt her.

"Jesus." He examined her in minute detail, looking for a bump or a bruise. "I'm sorry. I didn't mean—"

"Get off me."

She smacked his hands away, bristling with impatience and struggling to roll over and get up on her own power. Screw that. Dawson lunged up first, hauling her with him—God, he'd forgotten how small she was—and didn't let go until he was sure she had her feet back under her. The babbling continued.

"Are you okay, baby?" He ran his hand over her bare shoulder again but saw no outward signs of damage, but you just never knew. Could he have torn her rotator cuff or something? "Maybe you should get checked out while we're here."

Arianna planted her palms on his chest and leaned into a push that nearly slammed him against the wall. "I said, *Get off me!*" She divided her glare equally between him and Andrew. "Aren't things bad enough without you two clowns brawling like this is a playground?"

Dawson flinched with increased shame, but Andrew kept right on trucking, one dark eyebrow on the rise as he stared at Dawson with open speculation. *"Baby?"*

Arianna pointed her manicured index finger at Andrew's nose. "Don't you start again—"

"What's, ah, going on in here?"

They all looked around as a guy wearing scrubs and god-awful orange Crocs strolled into the room. Nurse, doctor, physician's assistant, it was impossible to tell. All Dawson knew was that, judging from the suspicious and disapproving light in the dude's eyes, he was one second away from calling security.

Recovering quickly, Dawson smoothed his clothes and pretended he was calm. "Family discussion," he said idly. "Happens all the time."

The medical professional's gaze swung around to Andrew for confirmation.

Andrew produced a crooked smile. "You heard the man."

"Right." The guy narrowed his eyes and flashed warnings in all their directions—*Behave or I'll bounce you on your asses, Warner family or not*—before he came to the reason for his appearance. "Is there a Josh in here? Mr. Bishop wants to see you before the procedure."

Dawson stepped forward. "I'm Joshua," he said, because suddenly he was.

"I want to prepare you a little bit." The guy's expression sobered, slamming the door firmly shut on the possibility of any good news, at least for now. And here Dawson had thought he'd maxed out on the whole scared thing for the day, but no. "Mr. Bishop is awake and lucid, but his speech is a little garbled right now—"

A ripple of alarm made its way around the room, touching everyone.

"—and it's too soon to say how extensive the problem is, or how long it'll last. Okay? And the other thing is," he continued, "that we've got him prepped for surgery, so you know he's got an IV line and—"

"We understand." Dawson tried to keep the impatience out of his voice, but it was hard when he couldn't shake the terrible certainty that his father was down the hall dying while they were in here yakking. "Where is he?"

They all trooped after the guy and passed through the automatic metal doors into the Neuro-ICU itself. It didn't seem to have occurred to anyone else that Bishop had asked for Dawson and not the entire gang, and Dawson did not, for once, have the heart to do the vindictive thing and tell them all to get the hell out. Much to his surprise, his spite only went so far, and keeping Bishop's loved ones away at this crucial hour turned out to be a line even he wouldn't cross.

They passed several windowed and curtained rooms, all filled with people who looked to be in the kind of dire medical straits that required a priest, minister or rabbi—possibly all three—and then Dawson saw him, in the farthest room.

The nurse or whoever walked right in and beelined for the bed, but Dawson hung back, hovering in the open doorway. The others didn't even come that far. He almost wished he could duck behind them and send them in first. Once they made sure Bishop wasn't dying, not today, not yet, then Dawson would be happy to go in. If that made him a coward, then he was happy to paint his belly yellow right now.

The indecisive lingering might have gone on forever, but then, from the depths of the bed, Bishop turned his head and looked at him. Raising a shaky hand to beckon him closer, Bishop opened and closed his mouth. Once. Twice. Three times. Only a jumbled growl came out. On the fourth try, long about the time Dawson felt hot tears burning his eyes and an excruciating knot of pity and embarrassment collecting in his throat, Bishop produced something intelligible.

"Josh-a."

Still Dawson couldn't move. The awful shock of seeing this hospital room, the white-sheeted adjustable bed, the beeping monitors and instruments, the multiple IVs with tubes snaking down to the taped and gnarled back of Bishop's hand, and there, almost as an afterthought amongst all that medical stuff, the tiny old man with the white hair, was too much for Dawson. He was overcome with emotion and choked by a sob that wouldn't quite rise up and wouldn't quite slide down.

This whole time he'd thought he hated the old man. Huh. Yeah. Sure. Right now the only thought in his head was that if he could unstick his feet from the floor he'd run to the bed and beg his daddy not to die on him.

"Josh-a," Bishop said again, that hand still extended to him.

Something brushed by Dawson and squeezed into the room past him, jarring him just enough to look around, blink and recover some of his senses. Arianna was there, thinking faster than him, lightening the room and the situation the way she always did.

"I've got a few words for you, Bishop." She breezed right up to that bed like she visited hospitals and critical-care units every day of her life, the way Dawson imagined she'd greet Bishop if she ran into him in the rose garden and they stopped to admire a butterfly together. "You scared us half to death, you know that? Don't you do that again, okay?"

She took that outstretched hand and squeezed it, and then she leaned over the bed and hugged Bishop around the shoulders, kissing his forehead. She wasn't scared. And Bishop tilted his chin up and beamed at her as though she were the sun and the moon, the stars and the universe, all tucked into one beautiful hundred-pound package.

Dawson stared at the two of them.

"Did the doctors talk to you about your blockages?" Arianna continued. "They're about to run you into the O.R. and get you fixed up. I imagine they've got some Drano in there or something."

Bishop tried to smile, but things with his mouth weren't working that well at the moment, and he wound up with a lopsided grimace that was still a comfort to Dawson. Because his father was still here, still in there. That hadn't changed. The body may have been damaged a little, but a spirit like that would surely shine forever.

Arianna kissed Bishop's cheek again and soothed his forehead with rhythmic strokes of her hand. "So you need to focus on getting well soon, okay?" She lowered her voice to a conspiratorial whisper. "Aunt Arnetta is already running amok. While we were out there in the waiting room, she called Cook and asked her to fix her some cinnamon rolls for dessert tonight. We can't have that."

Bishop rumbled an indistinct warning and scrunched his face into a glower. No one within a five-mile radius of that expression could mistake that warning: *You damn well better make sure Arnetta Warner doesn't try anything sneaky while my back is turned.* For good measure, he shook his head darkly.

Arianna got the message. "I can only hold her off for

so long, Bishop. You're the only one who can handle that woman. So you get well. You got it?"

Bishop opened his mouth with painstaking effort. "Ga. It."

For the first time Arianna faltered, and her face crumpled, just a little. "Oh, Bishop," she murmured, sniffling.

But Bishop didn't have time for sentimentality now, and he turned his head toward the door again, his expression immovable, but his eyes fierce. That hand went out again. "J-Josh-a."

Arianna snapped back to attention and looked around, matching and probably exceeding Bishop in the ferocity department. "Joshua," she said, extending her own arm. Her voice was loud and clear as a bell forged from iron, and even with all his emotions gone haywire, Dawson didn't miss her determined use of his real name. "Your father would like to see you before he goes into his surgery."

So Dawson went. If Arianna could go into that room and touch Bishop, then so could he. If she could be brave, then so could he. If she could handle a crisis, then he damn sure wasn't going to cower in the doorway.

When he got to the bed, Arianna put her hand to his back to pull him closer. When he reached the point where closer would have put him under the blankets with Bishop, she kept her hand there, in the small of his back, and it was a warm hand, a hand infused with the quiet strength of a mountain. And swear to God, he felt a billionth of her strength flow into his body and he soaked it up, greedy and needy.

"Josh-a," Bishop said again, craning his neck to meet his gaze.

They stared at each other, each stricken with unwanted silence. Between the two of them, unsaid words accumulated and hovered, threatening to fall to the linoleum floor with a clatter.

For the first time since he and God parted ways, on that horrific day when the prison bars slammed shut against him for a crime he hadn't committed, Dawson sent up a real, fervent prayer: *Please, God, don't let this man die on the table. I'm begging you. Give me one more chance with him.*

And God, who must have been having a slow day, whispered to him.

Touch him, Joshua.

So Dawson took his father's hand.

And when Bishop squeezed it, long and hard, he squeezed back.

Chapter 8

The waiting started.

Arianna spent a lot of time trying not to count every second or wonder how Bishop's eighty-plus-year-old heart was holding up under the anesthetic. When that didn't work, she tried not to think of scalpels and needles, blockages and the possibility of stroke during the procedure. No luck with that, either. Ditto with trying not to think about where Dawson had disappeared to and what he must be going through this very second.

When the family—now joined by Andrew's wife, Viveca, and Eric's wife, Isabella, who'd cut short their zoo visit and dropped the children at home with the housekeeper—went down to the cafeteria for a late lunch, Arianna ducked out. She'd had vague thoughts of sticking around in case Dawson reappeared and fisticuffs broke out again, but why? Dawson was gone and Viveca and

Izzy, who could surely handle any Warner male–induced emergency, were there.

And the very last thing she needed, anyway, was to emotionally entangle herself any further with Dawson, the poster child for the kind of unreachable bad boy that any thinking woman should stay far away from. Seriously. Signing up to be a suicide bomber was a safer prospect than any further involvement of any kind with…him. Whatever his name was.

She went outside to the—big surprise—Reynolds Warner Memorial Garden and sat on a bench next to a pretty little stone fountain. Settling against the back, she tilted her face up to the sun's warmth, closed her eyes and tried to find enough peace to get her through the waiting.

It almost worked. After a few minutes, she felt some of the tension begin to ease from her kettledrum-tight shoulders, but that was when it happened.

"Is this seat taken?"

Him.

She stiffened into concrete again. For one foolish second, she thought of ignoring him, but that would just be ridiculous, and it wasn't like they were in second grade. No matter what else happened, she could act like the dignified woman she was and deal with him with grace and maturity.

The bastard.

Cracking her eyes open, she looked up. He towered over her, with a stack of two white Styrofoam clamshells in one hand and a couple cans of soda, one diet and one not, in the other. He looked flushed and possibly nervous but said nothing further and waited patiently for her decision.

A distant voice tried to talk sense to her. A smarter

version of herself, it stood on a faraway mountaintop and flapped its arms, and then in growing desperation tried flags, Morse code and smoke signals.

Leave him alone, dummy! You know he's not for you! This won't end well!

All of that was perfectly sensible and probably prescient.

Arianna was smart. She'd graduated from Yale Law. She should listen.

On the other hand, that guardian angel's voice was faint, and he was right there in all his moody, dark-eyed glory. They both needed a temporary distraction, and he'd brought food. As long as there was no greenhouse within walking distance, nothing could happen, right?

So, yeah, he could stay. But that didn't mean she had to be nice to him.

The decision made, she frowned at him with all the indifference she could manage, which was somewhere between zero and one-half gram.

"That depends. Are you planning to start any more fights today?"

"No."

"Do you have any more names I need to know about?"

Something in his face softened. If a person could smile without moving his lips, then he was doing it. "No."

"Is that food for me?"

"Yeah. Least I can do for knocking you down earlier."

At this reminder of his latest transgression against her, she narrowed her gaze. "Don't think I've forgotten. Or forgiven."

He nodded. "I don't blame you. Do you want me to leave?"

No. "Yes." She paused, giving him time to flush and

shift uncomfortably. "But it's safer to keep an eye on you since you're like a well-dressed tornado, wreaking havoc wherever you go."

"A well-dressed tornado?" He tilted his head, considering this and accepting it with a shrug. "I've been called worse."

"You deserved it—whatever it was," she said flatly.

This assessment didn't abash him in the least. "You're right. Can I sit down? Now that the food's cold?"

She flashed him a final warning look and moved her purse aside for him. "As long as you understand I'm going to talk to you. That's what people do when they eat together; they have a conversation. Can you handle that?"

"Yeah. I figure your nonstop chattering is a good distraction right now."

Hold up. She talked a fair amount, yeah, but she did not *chatter*—

He sat down, and her gathering outrage stalled in her throat.

Oh, no.

The bench had seemed like an adequate seating device for two to three people, but that was before *he* came along, crowding her and throwing off waves of heat scented with the earthy deliciousness of his cologne. Had he always been this big? Really? How did he make it through life trying to negotiate those shoulders around corners and through doorways?

"I don't chatter," she said sourly, for the record, acutely aware of his muscled arms and thighs and the brush of his silk sleeve against her bare arm.

"Sure you do." He passed her a container of food. "Here."

On cue, her belly rumbled with unexpected hunger.

Opening the clamshell with a swell of hope, she looked inside and discovered…a salad.

He, meanwhile, was about to dig into a loaded burger with great gusto.

"I want that," she said when the burger was one inch from his gaping mouth.

"You're lucky to get anything. Eat it. Women eat salad."

That kind of nonsense didn't need to be dignified, so she clasped her hands together in front of her heart and let her lower lip tremble. "Please," she whispered, "I'll do anything."

That did it. The huskiness of her tone made his eyes glaze for a second, and she could almost see the memories of last night scroll through his brain. To his credit, he snapped out of it quickly and handed over the burger with a wry smile and good grace.

"Impressive," he conceded.

"I know." She took a giant bite of the burger, which was cold but gooey.

"Does that routine always work for you?"

Laughing, she handed him a fry, just to make peace. "Usually."

That fry disappeared with a single chew and a gulp, leaving him free to focus all his considerable energy on her. "So you're a Warner, eh?"

"Not exactly."

"Close enough. Why didn't you mention it last night?"

Was he blaming her for that? She stared at him, longing with every molecule of her being to dump her burger upside down in his lap. "There's a lot we didn't get to last night."

Something dark glinted in his eyes, a wicked warning

that reminded her of all the things they'd done together in the dark and all the things he still wanted to do with her.

"There's a lot we did get to, Ari."

She ignored the yearning huskiness in his voice. "For example," she continued as though that sound she'd just heard was nothing more meaningful than a passing fly's buzz, "you didn't mention your family ties or your multiple names or your irrational desire to spill Warner blood."

Tension pulsed in his jaw. "First, I don't want to spill blood—"

"Much," she said darkly.

"—and second, it's not irrational."

Did he actually believe that? "You just want what's coming to you. Is that it?"

"Exactly."

"Did you ever think that maybe you want the wrong thing?"

His lips flattened down to a slash of annoyance and disbelief. "And what should I want instead of my birthright, pray tell?"

"Peace."

That got him. She knew it would. Floundering and silenced, he stared at her until he couldn't stare anymore. And then he looked away.

Fueled by her newfound righteous serenity—they both knew she was right, even if he wasn't willing to admit it—she worked on her burger.

He, meanwhile, stabbed at his salad with vindictive enthusiasm and worked on his argument. "Spoken like a pretty little princess," he said finally, "who grew up in a penthouse where her mommy and her daddy worshipped and spoiled her and she never knew anything *but* peace."

She had to smile because he was so funny. Unwittingly

funny, but still funny. Did he seriously think this gruff finger-pointing routine would make her scuttle into a corner and hide? "The thing about peace is—if you don't have it, you can make it."

That shut him up. Again.

Immensely satisfied, she took another bite or two of her burger.

He regarded her with utmost derision, as though she believed it was possible to live on sunshine, love and puppies. "Is life that easy for you? Just make peace?"

Maybe he didn't believe it, but she did. "It's that easy."

"Where did you come from?"

Arianna stilled.

Because he didn't say it like he wondered how she'd managed to escape and when the men would arrive with the nets to take her back to the facility. He said it with a hint of wonder and a flare of unwilling interest in his eyes. He said it as though she'd arrived in the nick of time, and he was damn glad she had.

And, God, she just couldn't think when he looked at her like that.

"Eat." She pointed to his salad, desperate to direct his interest somewhere else.

To her surprise, he did.

They ate in a companionable silence that was broken only when he held out the diet soda. "Don't even try it," she told him. Rolling his eyes, he kept the diet for himself and gave her the leaded version.

The sun shone, robins sang and splashed in the fountain, people came and went from nearby benches. And in that perverse way men had of doing things, especially after the bickering they'd just done, he calmed her down and brought her that peace she'd needed. Merely by sitting beside her with his quiet, solid energy.

Yeah. That was a problem.

And then a bigger problem reared its big, fat, ugly head.

He threw their trash away and then casually reached over to brush her breeze-blown hair away from her cheek, stroking her skin with those amazing fingers. It was the kind of instant-relaxation touch that melted her innards, and she couldn't bottle up her tiny sigh of pleasure.

Naturally he took advantage of her pathetic weakness and kept stroking. And she, fool that she was, kept letting him. For a minute. Then she found the strength to pull her face away and shoot him a sidelong frown.

"You really should stop touching me."

He hesitated, but she wasn't dumb enough to think the matter had been settled. Those fingers came right back, twining in her curls and then tucking them behind her ear. "It's hard for me not to touch you after last night. I feel like I have blanket permission to touch you. We can't put the genie back in the bottle."

God, how did he do it? Those hands were freaking amazing. If he kept up like this, she'd have a shouting orgasm in another minute, right here in public, and then fall, comatose, into a nap right on this hard bench.

Pissed off by his power over her, she jerked away. "You had permission last night. Today you're back to nowhere with me."

He didn't like this pronouncement, not if the immediate brow lowering was any indication. "You promised you'd remember," he said, as though there was a snowball's chance in a Sahara summer that she'd forget.

"And you promised you'd meet me at the pasta bar, but

you walked out, and that made me feel like a hooker on a corner downtown."

Whoa. She hadn't meant to be quite *that* honest.

"Don't do that to yourself," he said vehemently. "What happened with us had to happen. There was no stopping it." His eyes went all sad on her, and with all the earnestness of a convicted murderer arguing his case for getting into heaven to St. Peter, he said, "I'm sorry I left, Arianna. I'm *sorry.*"

She turned her head, determined to remain unmoved even though her vulnerable heart was beginning to ache.

And then he played dirty.

"One day real soon, Ari," he said, in the gentlest voice imaginable, "we'll have to talk about this some more. We need to come to an understanding."

That anger surged again, hotter this time because it was directed inward. How could she blame him for trying to get laid again? He was a man; it was what they did—that, and make empty promises. She was the stupid one here, not him.

But it was easier to turn that fury outward than it was to own it.

"Understand this," she said. *"Keep your hands off me."*

Before he could say anything, his cell phone rang.

Hurtled back to the crisis with the force of a catapult, they exchanged a look of mutual wide-eyed panic—*Oh, God. Bishop*—and then he fished the phone out of his pocket and raised it to his ear.

"Yeah?" He listened, his gaze glued to hers, and she prayed until he hung up, his expression unreadable.

"Tell me," she said.

Dawson's face contracted, stopping her heart, but then

he let out a sharp bark of laughter. "He…came through with flying colors. It looks…good."

She was afraid to let herself believe it. "Really?"

He nodded.

Relief hit her hard. Joyous, overwhelming, breathtaking relief. It bubbled up her throat and she opened her mouth, thinking she'd laugh with Dawson.

That was when, to her complete horror, she burst into tears.

Hold up…was she crying?

Oh, man.

Paralysis struck him down. Normally, he had zero patience with emotional women, and he put them in the same category as malaria and buffalo stampedes: things to avoid at all costs.

But that was women.

This was Arianna, the woman who had, throughout this crisis, shown the coolheaded calm of General Eisenhower on D-day. Arianna was a rock, and he'd bet his next ten years of freedom that she rarely cried.

What the hell did he do now?

He couldn't ignore it, even though her ducked head told him she was embarrassed and wanted to hide. Not when the sight of those sparkling tears made him want to howl with sympathetic grief.

Yeah. Clearly he'd lost his freaking mind. "Don't cry," he told her.

Actually, he didn't tell her so much as he ordered her.

"I'm not." Turning away, she swiped at her eyes and sniffled.

"Don't bullshit me." His voice sounded gruffer by the second, probably because his rising desperation was making him crazy. If Arianna was upset, he felt the driving urge to fix it. Whatever it took to put the light back in those eyes. "What's wrong? The old man's going to be okay—"

"I know."

"So what's this about?"

"I'm relieved."

She offered up a watery smile, but he saw it for the deflection it was.

"Yeah? And?"

The questions put a dent in her defenses. Her bottom lip quivered for a minute, but then her mouth firmed. "This whole thing. It…reminded me of my father."

He smoothed back her hair—she didn't stop him—and asked gently, "What happened to him?"

That gaze turned back to him, the bleakest of Arctic winters. "He had a brain aneurism a few years ago. Died on the table."

Oh, man. He hated to think of her suffering on that terrible day.

"I'm sorry."

Nodding, she put the past firmly behind her and resumed her agenda with the levelheaded practicality he'd begun to see as her trademark.

"I didn't have any more time with my father. But you've got a second chance with yours. What're you going to do with it?"

No interview in his life had ever felt this tense, or this important.

"I need to figure that out, don't I?"

"You're not going to waste it, though," she said.

There was no question in there, but she waited anyway, giving him the chance to come correct and do the right thing. And he'd discovered, all through this long morning, that where Arianna was concerned, he wanted to…he wanted to…he wanted to come correct, yeah, but that wasn't all.

He wanted to…be better…at everything.

Better man. Better son. Better human being.

Otherwise, how could he—

What? How could he *what?*

His mind's eye squinted, peering in the distance, but he couldn't see that far. All he knew was that he wanted something from her, and it was only partially about sex. The rest was unknown, but he was still determined to get it.

"No," he told her. "I'm not going to waste it."

"Good."

A gleam of satisfaction appeared in her eyes, but she didn't gift him with the whole smile this time. Reserving judgment, probably. Smart girl, but man, he wanted that smile, especially after the tears. He wanted all her smiles, but there was time for that later.

She held her hand out to him. "Let's go see your father."

Emotion tiptoed up on him all of a sudden, catching him by surprise, and he stalled, not sure what to do with all the blessings in a life he'd considered cursed.

His father wasn't dead or dying; they both had a second chance. The sky was blue, and he was a free man. And Arianna, the woman who was light-years above him in every imaginable way, and who'd told him not ten minutes ago not to touch her, was voluntarily offering him her soft little hand.

If there was something better than this in the universe, he didn't think his heart was strong enough to behold it.

He tightened his lips and wished his nostrils would stop flaring, but of course her sharp eyes saw it all and softened with understanding.

That put him over the edge. He didn't give himself a chance to think.

Taking her hand, he reeled her closer across the bench. Some of his sudden intensity must have shown in his face, because she stiffened and turned her head, straining to get away. His pride should have kicked in about then, but his need was greater. Breathing her in, that wonderful scent of warm, healthy Arianna, he let his nose lead him to her cheek, where he hovered and imagined some of the connection they'd shared last night was still there.

"Please," he whispered, just brushing her ear with his lips. "This one time."

Her body eased, just enough, and he knew that was all the permission he'd get. So he kissed her on the cheek, a lingering kiss that channeled his gratitude, desire and all the other bewildering things he was beginning to feel about this woman.

It was the best kiss of his life.

Back up in the recovery area, the scene was exactly as Dawson had expected, but still an unpleasant shock—like knowing you'll get buzzed if you mess around with a plug, but sticking your finger in anyway.

The cast was assembled; all the players in his life, right there before him.

Bishop slept on the bed, surrounded by the machines and whatnot. Andrew and Viveca hovered on one side of the bed, Arnetta on the other. Eric and his wife, Isabella, huddled in the far corner, murmuring together.

Walking into the room with them together already, he felt that nose-pressed-up-against-the-glass sensation of non-belonging he'd felt almost since he had memory.

He didn't belong at the sickbed, or at Heather Hill. Nor did he belong in prison. Hell, why not face the big picture? He didn't belong anywhere on earth that he'd yet discovered, and he was sick of it.

On the other hand…he was also sick of his woe-is-me routine.

He'd had a few rough patches, yeah, but today was a new day and he'd always believed in engineering his own fate. His relationship with his father was in the toilet, but he could change that. He didn't have a place where he belonged, but he could change that. He didn't feel like a Warner, but that would change, too.

He wasn't going to sulk his way through the rest of his life.

So. No time like the present to start sunny-siding things.

Shooting a quick sidelong glance at Arianna, who dimpled in sympathy, he squared his shoulders and started acting like a grown-up.

"How is he?" he asked Andrew.

Andrew gave him one of those cool-eyed assessments. "Groggy. Stable."

Nodding, Dawson turned to Viveca, who was a stone-cold looker. Casual in her tank top and cargo pants, she had a curvy body that had probably dropped Andrew straight to his knees, and a keen intelligence shining in her dark eyes. He knew instinctively that this woman didn't suffer fools. She also kept Andrew on his toes.

"I'm Dawson Reynolds," he told her, extending his hand.

"Viveca Warner." She shook with a firm grip and studied him with a reporter's open curiosity. "You look like Reynolds," she said, angling her head for a closer look and ignoring Andrew's low rumble of displeasure. "You've got his nose and mouth."

That was something he'd never heard before. "Is that good or bad?"

Viveca flashed him a wry grin. "We'll see."

Moving on, he focused on Eric's wife, who was shorter and plumper in an all-American-girl type of way. Up until now, he hadn't been aware that orange and pink went together, but something about her flowery dress suited her sunny smile as she stuck out her hand.

"I'm Isabella," she told him. "Welcome to the family."

"For God's sake," Eric muttered.

"Ah." Dawson divided his gaze between the two of them. "Thanks."

And then, with no further warning, she pulled him in for a rib-shattering hug. Under normal circumstances, he'd give himself a moment to enjoy close body contact with a beautiful woman, but the warning glint in Eric's eye told him not to appreciate anything about Isabella too much.

So he pulled back and smiled. "I appreciate it."

The introductions and niceties thus observed, he nodded once to Arnetta, who still looked dazed and confused, and then focused on Andrew, the Warner leader. "So," he said.

Andrew folded his arms across his chest and raised his brows, imperious through and through. It was funny to think that they shared a father. What did they have in common that Dawson hadn't yet realized? Ears? Teeth? Arrogance?

"So," Andrew replied.

"So," Dawson continued, "I know we're not going to be BFFs or anything—"

Andrew snorted with unmistakable agreement.

"—but we are half brothers—"

"We'll need a paternity test to settle that issue."

"—and we both want what's best for Bishop."

"Do we?"

Okay. So much for extending the olive branch of peace; Dawson was starting to get seriously pissed off. What was with the belligerent tone? Could the brother not even meet him a quarter of the way? Would that be so hard?

Dawson planted his feet wide, ready for another fight if another fight was coming, and tried again even though he longed to pop some sense into Andrew. Part of the problem was that they had, in fact, been best friends back in the day, or so he'd thought. The *forever* part had long ago fallen by the wayside, but wasn't there anything salvageable from the relationship?

"Yeah," he said, trying not to sneer. "We both want what's best for Bishop, and I don't want to argue with you over his sickbed, *Scooter*—" Andrew's narrowed eyes told him he didn't like the use of his childhood nickname, but screw him "—so maybe we should work on a truce."

There. He'd made his peace offering, and he'd meant it. If Andrew wanted to spit in his face in front of this audience, then that was his choice. But no one could say Dawson hadn't tried, and tried hard.

He waited.

Andrew glowered. Eric leaned against the far wall and studied his nails, looking bored. Isabella coughed nervously. Arnetta smoothed Bishop's sheets over his chest. At Dawson's side, Arianna was absolutely still, as though her own fate hung in the balance.

Finally, Andrew peeled his fierce glare away from Dawson and looked to his wife. Viveca gave him a tiny wink and tilted her head exactly one millimeter in Dawson's direction. This seemed to turn the tide, because Andrew rolled his eyes and looked back to Dawson.

"Truce." Andrew's face couldn't have been sourer if

he'd drunk a lemon-pickle juice cocktail with a vinegar chaser.

"Great."

"Great."

They stared laser strikes at each other, neither blinking.

This might have gone on for the rest of the day, but Arianna emitted a discreet cough that sounded an awful lot like the word *shake*.

He got the message and stuck his hand out, extending it over Bishop's prone body on the bed. Andrew eyed him for a minute and then reached out.

They shook.

That was extraordinary enough. But then Andrew shocked the hell out of him. "Why don't you, ah, stay at the house while you're in town? Bishop would want that."

Dawson prided himself on his poker-faced arctic coolness in most situations, but his jaw still hit the floor. Collecting himself took a while; his thoughts took another couple beats to crystallize.

This wasn't the most gracious invitation he'd ever received, and he was betting Andrew planned to count the silver before and after Dawson's visit. Another issue was Dawson's raw pride, which demanded that he throw Andrew's charitable offer back in his face and tell him to go screw himself. Twice.

On the other hand…

He'd waited for this moment. To be welcome. To belong. To have a place.

And it wasn't about the house. It was about the feeling and the need, much as he wished he didn't need a damn thing in life.

Not that he was fooling himself. He wasn't truly

welcome any more than poison ivy was welcome at a Boy Scout campout. And more than likely, they were only offering him the crawl space over the garage or a corner of the wine cellar in the basement.

But it was a start.

And Arianna was staying at Heather Hill. God knew he wanted to be as close to her as he could get.

So he swallowed his squawking pride and didn't try to block his unexpected smile. "I'll do that," he told Andrew. "Thanks."

Chapter 9

At Heather Hill that evening, Dawson, who'd been showing more and more signs of civility as the day went on, as though he had not, in fact, been raised by cursed and rabid wolves, escorted Arianna to the door of her cottage, where she was staying.

Shadows had lengthened across the porch, which was now a cool mecca against the sun's remaining heat. She almost wished they could spend more time together. Maybe sit on the wicker love seat and just hold hands, decompressing together after their traumatic day, or maybe go for a dip in the pool.

It would be so nice.

On the other hand, she could hardly relax when that disquieting light had begun to glow so brightly in his eyes. Now that Bishop was out of the woods, she knew her reprieve was up and Dawson wanted to press his case.

She tried to be indifferent, but the responsive swoop of pteranodon-sized butterflies in her belly didn't help.

At the front door, she gave him an impersonal smile and kept her voice brisk. "Thanks for walking me down. You didn't have to."

That dark gaze held hers. "And you didn't have to take me back to the hotel to grab my bags and then bring me here."

"Well, I—" Fishing her keys out of her bag, she fumbled for the right one, dropped them and cursed her nervous clumsiness when he picked them up. It was no surprise at all when he used the opportunity to shift closer. "Thanks." She took the keys and unlocked the door as fast as she could. "I'm trusting you not to cause a fight up at the big house."

"Wouldn't dream of it. I wish you'd have dinner with me."

Damn it. They'd covered this ground already in the car. "I told you. No thanks."

"What about breakfast tomorrow before we go back to the hosp—"

"No."

"Maybe we can just sit out here and talk, order a pizza—"

"No." God. His patient reasonableness was seriously making her crazy. Why wouldn't he drop it? She had the terrible certainty that he'd stand there and methodically ask her to share every meal between now and Thanksgiving with him if she didn't make her escape. "I told you—we don't have anything to talk about."

"I think we need to talk about last night—"

"Fine." She let the screen door bang shut, because clearly she wouldn't escape until they had this stupid and pointless conversation. "Last night. Best sex of my life.

Then you walked out on me, and I got the message loud and clear: you're not up for any kind of relationship that even peripherally requires you to think about the woman's feelings. So let's leave it at that, shall we? Thanks for screwing me so great last night. Have a nice life."

Propelled by her anger, she wheeled around to leave and got nowhere.

"You may have been screwing." His gentle hand on her arm kept her close. "But I was making love."

That was a low blow designed to hit any woman squarely in her foolish heart, and it annoyed her even though she knew better than to believe him. "How touching. Too bad you blew it."

"I did mess up by leaving last night," he said evenly. "But I was coming back for you. And that's what I would have done later this morning if Bishop hadn't gotten sick."

"And how were you going to find me? Telepathy?"

Judging by the irritated twist of his lips, he didn't appreciate the sarcasm. He reached into his pocket and produced a royal-blue something, which he held up between his first two fingers.

Intrigued despite herself, she snatched it and glared down.

Oh, God.

It was a cocktail napkin from the party last night. With her cell phone number on it. She stared at it, then at him. Her brain, meanwhile, left the building. "What's this?" she asked blankly.

His eyes gleamed with predatory satisfaction. "It's a little piece of information I paid a hundred dollars for last night. One of the party planner's minions checked the clipboard for me and passed it along."

Well, so what if he'd taken a little initiative? She

would not be impressed. "It's hard to get good help these days."

"Seeing my father threw me out of whack last night, and I needed to get it together. I wasn't ready to explain it all to you." He paused, a flush creeping up his neck to his cheeks. "I'm not proud of it."

Yeah. She could see that, and also what it cost him to admit it to her.

"But I wasn't about to let you get away just because I had a few issues I needed to work out."

"Why didn't you try to explain?"

"Explain what?" His palms-up gesture all but screamed frustration. "*What?* We've already established that you're too good for me—"

"That's ridiculous."

"—and that you could do better than me. What was I supposed to do? Hit you with the information that I was a convicted rapist who spent years in prison? Or should I have started with my other shameful secret, which is that my birth father pawned me off on my adoptive father, both of whom washed their hands of me? That's the kind of thing you want to discuss at the pasta bar in the middle of a party with the fantastic woman you just met, isn't it?"

Last night wasn't the time for all that, no, but that wasn't the issue here, and she wasn't going to let her empathy sidetrack her. "Do you ever get sick of yourself and your woe-is-me routine?"

His lips peeled back from his teeth in a close cousin to a snarl, but she wouldn't pull her punches, not when he needed to hear this and she needed to say it.

Using her whiniest voice, she went for the jugular. "*Poor me, I went to prison. Poor me, my father hates me. Poor me, I'm not good enough for anything.* Does all that bitterness ever get on your nerves? Because it's sure gotten on mine."

Cursing, he looked away, back toward the main house, wondering why he'd come down here, no doubt. By his sides, his big hands clenched and unclenched into bigger fists, and if he'd lunged for her throat and begun to throttle her, she wouldn't've been the least surprised.

But then he did surprise her.

"Yeah," he said, turning back. "I'm sick of it. And I'm done with it."

Oh, how she wished that were true. Because this one man had more raw potential, more character and strength than probably anyone she'd ever met. If only he knew it. If only she could tell him. But the last thing she needed to do, ever, was open the door for him to come into her life and hurt her worse than he already had.

What was the saying? Fool me once and all that? Well, he'd fooled her once, and one chance was all he'd get with her. She'd had enough of men who said one thing and did another, thanks.

Besides. Her life was currently as big a quagmire as his was, and neither one of them was ready for a relationship as complex as the one they seemed to be developing. Sex was a big part of it, yeah, but an emotional connection was growing with each second they spent together, and she couldn't have that.

Emotional connection plus bitter bad boy equals disaster for Arianna.

No deal.

"Done with the self-pity," she echoed. "Glad to hear it. Have a nice life."

Again she turned to go inside, and again she got nowhere, but this was worse. This time he put his hand on hers, where it rested on the brass knob, and God, all that electric chemistry ran through her body, potent as a double shot of whiskey.

"Here's the thing," he said, and his low murmur made her shiver, as though he'd swirled his tongue up and down the curve of her spine. "I'm all about rebuilding things that're broken and correcting mistakes I've made. I want to do that with you."

She snatched her hand away, her growing agitation making her jittery. But he would not get to her. She wouldn't let him. "Too late."

Deep in his dark eyes, that quiet gleam of determination intensified. "I don't believe that."

"No?" Well aware that something inside her had snapped and a devastating confession was roaring up her throat, eager to be said despite all her best intentions, she didn't bother keeping the volume down. "Well, believe this: the second I laid eyes on you, I wanted you."

He took a sharp, surprised breath, which should have been her clue to shut the hell up, but hey, why not aim for utter and complete humiliation?

"And letting go of your hand last night was really, *really* hard. How ridiculous is that? But I didn't want to let you go, and the second I did, I started aching for you."

"Aching?" he echoed, looking stunned.

"Yeah, *aching*. You want to know where?"

He stilled. Waited.

Shut up, Arianna. Just shut the hell up before you make things—

"Here." She rubbed her hand over her skirt, down between her thighs, and up over her breasts. "Here."

He made a strangled sound and swallowed convulsively.

"And here." She touched her heart.

"Jesus," he muttered.

"You're doing something to me—you *affect* me—and I'm not ready for it."

Wide-eyed silence.

Brilliant, Arianna. Nothing like those soul-deep confessions to drive men away. Great. Well, time to wrap this conversation up. "You're not going to hurt me again."

"I don't plan to."

"How comforting. You didn't plan to last night, either, did you?"

"Last night I didn't know..." He trailed off and scrubbed his hand over his head, struggling to hold something back.

"You didn't know what?"

Unsmiling, he met her gaze again, and there was something in his expression that was so disquieting, so relentlessly powerful and *hot,* that she had to put her hand on the door again or risk being bowled over backward.

"I didn't know that I could feel this way about a woman."

What? What did that mean? What was he telling her? "How is that?"

"Like I would crawl through lava to see her smile."

"Don't." Desperate to appeal to his sense of fair play—she knew he had one buried in there somewhere—she resorted to begging. Anything to escape without further damage. "Please don't do this to me."

But he'd put his hands on her waist and wasn't listening. "Arianna."

"Don't," she tried again, and again after that. It didn't work. On her third *don't,* he covered her mouth with his.

What a liar she was; she knew it as soon as he kissed her. She could not shut him out of her life, even though she knew she should. She could not pretend that last night was a one-time-only occurrence. At this moment, she couldn't even dredge up the rudiments of why she wanted to.

All she wanted was *this.*

His tender lips on hers, his tongue deep in her mouth and hers in his.

Croons of satisfaction vibrated in his chest, and he gripped her closer, ruining her with his urgency and his desire, making her want things that were bad for her and didn't truly exist anyway. He wasn't the man she needed him to be—not yet—but God, she could pretend for another minute.

So she didn't resist when he cupped her butt in his big hands and ground that rigid erection against her. "God," she said, panting, because this man, and no other, made her mouth water, her brain freeze and her heart yearn for the impossible. "More. I want more."

Reaching up, she sank her fingers in the cottony fluff of his hair, bringing him tighter, closer. He tasted minty and comforting, familiar and disconcerting, and like her salvation and her ultimate destruction, all wrapped together in one body.

Yes. Yesss.

"Arianna." He ran his lips down the side of her neck, licking her overheated skin and lifting her off her feet. "Please."

Apparently she'd already decided with no input from her dazed brain. Crazed now, dizzy with lust, she reached for the bottom of his shirt, ready to get it out of her way. He laughed, the sound hoarse and triumphant. Even that didn't put the brakes on. Only when she felt the flaming heat from his velvety skin did reality rear its ugly head and show its gargoyle face, insisting that she see it.

What? God, *what* was she doing? She was not this stupid. She refused to be.

"No." She broke away and wished she'd put a little more bite in that *no.*

Sure enough, the whispered word had no discernible effect. His lips hunted her down, following as she turned her head, catching her again for another starved taste. And she…yeah, she let him, because she was weak, her desire was strong, and she'd only managed to grow about half a backbone where he was concerned.

But she was working on it.

"No." This time, she said it in a range audible to human ears. He paused, blinking in confusion, and she used the moment to her advantage. "No." She pulled back. *"No."* She slammed her palms against his chest and shoved him with all her might, which backed him up a full millimeter.

"Arianna—" he began, frustration rolling off his body in tsunami-sized waves.

"We're not doing this." She fumbled with the door for the umpteenth time and made it, for the first time, over the threshold. Just so he fully got the message, she ran the back of her hand over her mouth, swiping his kiss away the way she'd do if she kissed a muddy leech. "You broke trust with me last night. That's it. I don't need any more men in my life that I can't trust. Been there, done that. Sorry."

That, he heard loud and clear. His face contracted, and it didn't look like the irritation of a man who'd really wanted to get laid and now wouldn't. It looked like the abject despair of a man who'd fought his way to rainbow's end only to be denied the pot of gold.

"How can I get the trust back?"

Great question. Too bad she didn't have any answers.

"You can't," she told him.

The second Arianna hit the porch in the morning, late for the trip to the hospital as part of Bishop's welcome-home party, it hit her: the wondrous, delicious, welcome smell of hot chocolate.

But where—

Snuffling around, reminding herself of a bloodhound, she looked and…there it was! On the little wicker side table. Hot chocolate! In a white paper to-go cup, sitting next to a white paper bag that could only hold some type of delicious bakery treat.

Hurrying over, she snatched the bag up, totally understanding how strangers with sweets lured children into cars. Inside was a chocolate croissant, buttery fresh and flaky—

Wait. There was a card, with a single handwritten *A,* for *Arianna,* on the envelope.

Oh, no.

This was terrible. Only one person would make this kind of effort for her—the one person she needed to avoid: Dawson. Joshua. Whatever his name was.

Well, that did it. No way could she eat this, notwithstanding her stupid stomach, which was now rumbling hopefully. She would throw all of this away. Yes. That's what she would do.

With a guttural noise that would embarrass her when she remembered it later, she shoved half the croissant into her mouth, smacking like a cow chewing her cud.

Oh, man. Better than sex.

Taking another massive bite—in for a penny, in for a pound, right?—she read the card, which was written in a spare hand with slashes and long tails rather than loops.

Dear A—

One of the things I'd like to know about you is what you eat for breakfast. Until you tell me, I'll have to guess. I'm an oatmeal guy, but that doesn't seem right for you. I do know that you're a chocoholic, so I hope the croissant is a good start.

Other things I'd like to know about you:

What you've done every day of your life up until now;

Where you got your iron core of strength from; and

Your favorite television show.

"Oh, God."

Licking her fingers, she put the remaining bite of the croissant down. Eating, it turned out, was impossible when you were too stunned and heartsick to breathe.

Back to reading the note, not that it was a good idea to finish the damn thing.

Can I tell you something?

No way. The last thing she needed was any more of his confessions contaminating her brain. She was going to march inside and flush this note down the toilet right now.

I can't get you out of my mind.

Yours,
Dawson

One reading wasn't enough, so she read it again. And again.

He just killed her, touching her with his thoughtfulness and vulnerability. Why did she read the stupid note? *Why?* Well, she'd read it, but that didn't mean she had to keep it. No. She'd tear it up and put it in the recycling bin.

She tucked it into her purse.

Jerk. Why was he doing this to her?

Well. She'd read and kept the note and eaten the croissant, but at least she hadn't drunk the hot chocolate. See? She could resist him, after all. As long as she stood firm on one tiny issue, she was good.

Newly confident, she took two long strides to the porch steps.

Hah. Easy as pie.

On the third step, she looped back around, snagged the cup and took a long swig. Delicious. Damn him.

That afternoon, Dawson sat on the library sofa, which unfortunately put him in the direct path of Bishop's glare, and tried not to fidget. Maybe this whole visit thing wasn't such a hot idea, especially since the temporary peace they'd established before the procedure yesterday seemed to have gone up in smoke.

The old man had been home from the hospital for about an hour, which was enough time for him to commence being mad at the world. Sitting on the love seat next to Arnetta, he'd hated, in no particular order, the Welcome Home sign Arnetta had hung over the front door, the cheery flowers and the boxes of sugar cookies, his favorite. Also on his shit list: Andrew, Eric and their wives, all of whom had fussed over him once too often and been banished from the room in punishment.

"Good luck," Andrew muttered to Dawson, as they were filing out. "You're going to need it."

"No shit, Sherlock," Dawson hissed out of the side of his mouth. "Too bad they didn't send us home with a tranquilizer dart for the old guy."

Andrew snorted and Eric laughed outright. For a minute the three of them shared a moment—Dawson was reminded of the time Bishop had caught them trying to transfer some of Eric's fish from the lush saltwater tank into the swimming pool, just to see what they would do—and it was so much like the old days that Dawson felt a sharp pang of nostalgia.

Man. He almost wished—

Some unspoken and invisible signal zapped them all at the same time, snapping them out of it. They seemed to realize the slippery slope of being nice to each other and looked away, embarrassed. Dawson watched them disappear down the hall with an unexpected lump in his throat.

Not cool, man. Not cool at all.

Then they were gone and only he and Arnetta were left to absorb the brunt of Bishop's considerable temper.

The old man was in a foul-ass mood.

The glaring continued while Dawson tried to remain placid.

"Go home, Josh-a," Bishop told him, a dismissive hand flap tacked onto the end of his sentence just in case Dawson didn't get the message. "Bye."

Arnetta tutted and shot Dawson an apologetic look, which was funny since she'd never been that big a fan of her late husband's bastard son number two. "Bishop," she said, rubbing his thin shoulder, "you don't mean that."

While Dawson appreciated the attempts at diplomacy, they were pointless. "Of course he means it, Arnetta.

But I'm not leaving. I'm staying at Heather Hill now, Bishop."

"Why you come back?" The old man's brows dropped to a fuzzy and intransigent line above his flashing eyes. Dawson almost laughed. It was wild the way Bishop's spirit was still so clearly there and undamaged, despite the speech problems that would require therapy. "Make fun of me tease? Cause trouble?"

Fair questions.

Dawson shrugged and tried to put his former life's purpose in twenty-five words or less. "I came back to get what's coming to me: my place in the family. If that caused a little trouble, I didn't really care. But now—" His face flushed and he swallowed back a bit more of that unwanted emotion that kept throwing him off. "I thought I'd stick around a while and make sure you go to therapy and take it easy."

Uh-oh. Wrong thing to say. Big time.

Bishop's lips went hard and flat, and he cracked them open just enough to speak another mangled sentence. "You feel sorry for me pity. Get—"

"No, I don't."

"—out gone. Bye-bye."

Dawson started to get the picture. He should have realized sooner that no man, especially a proud and stubborn old fart like Bishop, who'd run this household since before Noah started collecting animals two by two, would want people either helping him or feeling sorry for him. Dawson understood; God knew he'd feel the same way if it were him.

"I don't feel sorry for you, old man." This wasn't entirely true, but what else could he say? "I'm here to make sure you get back to a hundred percent before Heather Hill falls down around your ears. We all know no one can run this place like you can, so I plan to kick your ass up one side and down the other if you don't follow your therapist's instructions."

Bishop's eyes widened with obvious surprise, and Arnetta said, "Oh, my."

Now that he had their full attention, Dawson leaned back and crossed one of his ankles on his knee. "And I want to make sure you don't terrorize the rest of the household while you're rehabilitating. Got it?"

Bishop shook his head, his expression stormy. "Don't need y-you. Y-you like me don't hate." Another head shake, violent with frustration at the garbled sentences. "Y-you hate me."

"I don't hate you, old man. But we've got a couple things to work out, don't we?"

Huh. *A couple things.* Big-time understatement.

Bishop seemed to take it as such, judging by the continued glowering.

Arnetta, meanwhile, divided her anxious attention between them, vibrating with the readiness to spring up and quash any violence that might break out. Maybe she was worried that any further interaction between father and son would lead to Bishop having another attack, but Dawson wasn't concerned. At the moment, the old man had enough iron in his spine to pick the whole mansion up and move it six inches to the left.

Bishop opened his mouth, determined to force out another sentence or two. "N-not 'old man.' Pops. Call me. Pops. Unner…unner…unnerstan?"

Was this funny, or what? It'd take more than a mere health crisis to take the stubborn out of Bishop. Dawson and Arnetta exchanged a tiny wry glance, and Dawson tried not to smile.

"Pops," he conceded.

Looking somewhat mollified, Bishop held up a shaky and gnarled index finger and wagged it at Dawson, then Arnetta, with a stern warning. "N-no pity sorry. Okay fine I'm." He scrunched his eyes closed and breathed in a long breath that was clearly meant to help him past this roadblock.

Then he tried again.

"I'm," he said with perfect clarity, "f-fine."

"I know," Dawson said.

Bishop turned to Arnetta for her agreement as well. Starchy as always, she hitched her chin up, as though she needed to keep the invisible crown on her head balanced.

"First of all," she told Bishop, "you're not in charge of this house. I am."

Both Bishop and Dawson snorted at this blatant lie, since everyone east of the Mississippi knew, and always had known, that while Arnetta was the money behind the Heather Hill operation, Bishop was the heart, but she ignored them both.

"Second," she continued, "I am perfectly capable of running this house until you're back up to speed—"

"Shit crap bull," Bishop muttered; Dawson swallowed his burst of laughter.

"—and third, you've taken care of all of us since dinosaurs roamed the earth—"

"Before," Bishop interjected.

"—so why don't you let us take care of you for once?"

This impassioned speech didn't make so much as a chink in Bishop's intransigence. "I. Run. House."

"Oh, fine," Arnetta huffed with exasperation. "You run the house. You, you, *you*. And if I find so much as one speck of dust on the furniture, I'm going to fire both you and the housekeeper. Does that make you happy?"

Apparently it didn't, because Bishop kicked that glare up into fifth gear, narrowing his eyes until it was a wonder he could see anything other than his own lashes. "No rolls junk."

For the first time, Dawson had no idea what the old man was talking about, but Arnetta obviously got his meaning loud and clear. You'd think she'd have a crick in her neck from keeping her royal nose stuck in the air for so long, but no. Damned if she didn't notch her chin a little higher.

"I will have Cook make me some cinnamon rolls if I want them. You couldn't stop me when you were at a hundred percent, and you won't stop me now."

O-ho. That old fight. Bishop had been trying to get the old girl to eat healthy since before Nixon thought about breaking into the DNC, and that tendency had no doubt intensified since her heart attack a few years ago.

"Not healthy bad." Bishop stared her down, his brows knit with fury. "I stop you."

This could go on for a while. Though Dawson was mildly interested in the outcome—if Batman and Wonder Woman went head-to-head, you wanted to see who emerged victorious—he had work to do and calls to make.

"I'll check in with you two later," he said.

They ignored him, and Arnetta was just getting wound up. "I'll thank you to remember that I'm—"

Chuckling, Dawson headed down the hall and around the corner.

And ran directly into Arianna.

Chapter 10

Instinct took over.

Spurred by the desire not to knock this poor woman down for the second time in twenty-four hours, and by the stronger desire to touch and hold her, even if it was for some trumped-up reason that should make his pride hang its head in shame, Dawson caught her.

They rocked together for a minute, long enough to regain their footing and for him to hear, and enjoy, the sharp hitch of her breath. She felt so freaking good, and he soaked up every unforgettable detail in that one second. The curve of her waist and the way the soft cotton of her dress slid over her toned flesh. Her compact strength, the mind-numbing heat of her. The delicious tropical scent of whatever she used on her hair and, finally, the silky slide of her bare arms as she stepped away.

"Sorry," he said.

Too flustered to look him in the eye, she covered by

tucking her hair behind her ear. "Maybe I should start wearing protective gear around you."

"I don't think that's necessary."

"I'm starting to feel unsafe." She hesitated, risking a quick peek up at him. "In more ways than one."

Dawson tried not to lose another little piece of himself to her, but there it went. Something about her unabashed vulnerability and honesty—and most everything else about her, frankly—had wormed its way into his blood and was now drumming a steady beat. There was no hidden agenda or game playing with this woman. What you saw was what you got, which was quite the refreshing change. Pretty much everyone else in his life, and certainly everyone here at Heather Hill, was duplicitous enough to work for some covert branch of the CIA, but not Arianna.

"I can see why you'd think that," he said softly. "But I'm planning to be much more careful with you in the future."

That made her bristle. "I'm not some fragile little—"

Arianna? Fragile? Yeah. And he planned to be the first human to flap his arms and fly to the sun and back. "I never said you were. All I'm saying is that if something is special to someone, he should take good care of it."

A slight widening of her gorgeous but wary eyes was the only reaction he got, and then she changed the subject. "Thanks for the, ah, hot chocolate this morning."

"You're welcome."

"And the croissant."

"My pleasure."

Ducking her head, she took a step toward the library. "I'll see you later."

"I wouldn't go in there if I were you." He put a hand on her arm to stop her, his urgency fueled by a ten-percent desire to give Bishop and Arnetta some privacy, and a ninety-percent desire to keep Arianna around for as long as possible. "The old folks are bickering."

"So what else is new?"

"It reminds me of the way he was with Mama, actually."

"Oh." Concern flickered in her eyes. "That must be hard."

"Yeah, well." He shrugged, but there was no keeping it light, not when he was talking about Mama. "She's been gone a long time."

"She died when you were in college, right?"

The new tightness in his throat settled into a lump and started to grow. "Yeah."

"Diabetes, or—"

"Complications, yeah."

The natural urge was for him to glare her into silence—he didn't make a habit of chitchatting about Mama's death and the subsequent beginning of the roughest time of his life—but Arianna wasn't asking out of idle curiosity. He'd be willing to bet she cared about him even if she'd rather die than admit it. Since his most fervent wish was for them to reestablish and grow their relationship into something, even if he wasn't quite sure what the *something* would look like, there was no time like the present to start opening up.

A little.

But only if she met him halfway.

So he sat on a carved bench facing the long hall's windows and gave it a shot. "Have you got a minute?"

"I don't—" She eyeballed the bench with open suspicion, probably remembering the first time they'd occupied a seating device together. Then she looked up and down the hallway, possibly calculating the nearest exits and relative proximity of others in the house, and made up her mind. She sat, much to his unreasonable joy. "Sure."

Scrubbing his hand across his jaw, he gave her the abridged version. "Mama died. Bishop fell apart and got depressed. I fell apart and started drinking and partying."

She nodded with complete understanding. "Your mother was the heart of the family. Mothers usually are."

"She was the only thing keeping me and Bishop from ripping each other's heads off, that's for sure." The memories were never far away, and they came back now in a swirling rush. Mama making his Spider-Man costume for Halloween; Mama letting him lick the pound cake batter off the beaters; Mama spanking his butt when he talked back, which was never with her but often with Bishop. "But with her gone, I don't think we knew how to deal with each other. His depression got worse and my drinking got worse. And then one Christmas, it all blew up."

"He told you he wasn't your father."

"You got it," he said, wrapping the bitterness around him like a down comforter on winter's coldest night. Because what else was he supposed to do? Show the world how hurt he was? How that one hurtful moment had ruined who he was and turned him into someone he'd never wanted to be? Hell, no. If he didn't have his pride, what was left?

That was his position, and he'd stuck to it for all these long and lonely years.

Until Arianna looked at him with those shining eyes and asked, "It hurt, didn't it?"

To his utter shame, a trembling began in his chin, and it stopped only when he twisted his lips and bit the inside of his cheek hard enough to draw blood. That sharp pain cleared his mind and gave him the control he needed. "Yeah. It hurt. I hadn't known I was adopted. It was… hard to find out like that."

"I guess so."

"The funny thing was, I was always Mama's, even though she didn't give birth to me. But I was never Bishop's. He never wanted me."

Arianna didn't buy it. He could tell by the open skepticism in her narrowed eyes that she didn't want to think ill of her beloved Saint Bishop.

"Is it possible he loved you but didn't know how to show—"

"No," he said flatly.

Sitting right in the crosshairs of her pure brown gaze, he had no choice other than to tell the truth, even though it was always so much easier to nurse his hurt. "I'm sure he tried," he admitted, the best he could do.

"It wasn't enough?"

"Let's just say that Bishop and I never fit together like a hand in a glove."

This time she conceded the point, her eyes clouding over on his behalf. "I'm sorry." To his surprise, she reached out a hand and sank it into the hair at his nape, giving him a caress that was probably supposed to comfort but also served to remind him of the magic that happened when they touched each other. "I'm sorry."

"Jesus." He couldn't keep his breath from spiking or a shudder from rippling through him. "You're pretty good with those mixed messages, Ari, you know that?"

Brilliant, jackass. Way to kill the mood.

Right on cue, she stiffened and started to move away. Catching that soft hand before she could escape, he leaned in, desperate to kiss her. Screw it. He might as well lay it all on the line.

"Come to my room with me, Arianna."

"No."

Damn it. He always had to push too hard, didn't he? Always had to ask too much. Like now. "Let me touch you."

"I can't."

"You want to."

"I want to."

He could see that. Desire radiated off her flushed skin, and her breath was choppy and short. Her lips were parted, her black pupils dilated. A textbook case of frustrated lust if ever he'd seen it, and he ought to know since he had a terminal case of it himself.

"Then why?" He ran his nose across her cheek, one inch from her sweet skin, breathing her in as much as he could. Nothing seemed more important than being close to her again, now. Sex was only part of it, and that was the scary thing, because sex had always been the be-all and end-all as far as he and women were concerned. "Tell me why."

"Because."

"Why?" He tried to keep the sharp edge out of his voice, but that was impossible in the grips of this kind of need.

"You've already hurt me once." She floundered, working hard to force the words out. "And this thing between us, it's—"

"What?"

"It's big." She slid down the bench and away from him. "What'll you do to me next time, if I let you?"

There wouldn't be a next time. Not if he had anything to say about it. But she didn't know that, and he'd given her no reason to take another gamble on him. "I get that you're afraid. I don't blame you. But this thing with us, this attraction, it's there. It's not going to go away if we ignore it. You know that. We're living on the same property, for God's sake.

"Not for long."

"For now, though."

His persistence seemed to tick her off, and a sudden gleam of anger flashed in her eyes. "Why are you doing this? You can't be hard up for women to have sex with. Are you?"

He didn't deny it. What would be the point? There were women he could have, yeah. The problem was, he'd had a hard time remembering any of their faces in the last couple of days.

"I don't want other women," he told her. "I want you."

For one heart-stopping second, he thought she was wavering. She stared at him, and he felt her hope and excitement, could almost smell them in the air. But then she shook her head in a firm no.

"Maybe you do," she said. "But I don't think you're finished wallowing in your bitterness, and I'm not ready for a relationship anyway. I don't think we'd do each other any good right now."

"I disagree."

"Maybe we do want each other." She took a stab at a brave, oh-what-does-it-matter grin as she stood, but the corners of her mouth refused to curl, and the grim determination in her eyes made smiling impossible anyway. "But we'll get over it."

He stood, too. "Arianna—"

She moved off and he put his hand on her arm to stop her.

And Andrew appeared around the corner.

All three of them froze with a kind of pregnant horror.

Yeaaah…awkward.

The brother's sharp eyes saw everything, in that annoying way they always did. Their flushed faces, the touch between them, the burning intensity. Arianna, recovering first and trying for that whole nothing's-going-on-here thing, stepped out of Dawson's grasp, but Dawson's defiant tendencies kicked into warp speed. He widened his stance and squared his shoulders. Yeah, he wanted Arianna, and he didn't care who knew it. Maybe King Andrew here wasn't too thrilled, but screw him. Who the hell was he? Self-appointed head of the family? Well, screw that, too.

"Everything okay here?" Andrew's voice had that false silky-calm quality that wouldn't fool a kindergartner. "Arianna?"

She flashed a bright smile, apparently determined to avert any pending violence. "Great." Patting Andrew on one cheek, she gave him a reassuring kiss on the other. Andrew's jaw flexed with clear annoyance at being handled, but that didn't break Arianna's stride any. "I was just leaving. So I'll see you both later."

She swept off down the hall, leaving a yawning wake of silent suspicion behind her. Dawson watched her go, deflating with each step she took. Andrew, meanwhile, swung all his narrow-eyed intensity around to Dawson.

"I think we need to have a talk," he said.

Yeah. They did, and Dawson knew it in the rational part of his brain. He and his beloved half brother here needed to clear the air on a whole host of topics, from Arianna to the unfortunate breakdown in their relationship all those years ago. Except that Dawson didn't feel like letting Andrew set the timetable, and he especially didn't feel like talking now, when he may have made a little headway with Arianna but now, thanks to this unwanted interruption, wouldn't.

"Later," he said, brushing past Andrew.

Andrew, naturally, was incapable of leaving well enough alone. He grabbed Dawson's arm in a hard grip that pissed Dawson off all the more. "What's going on with you and Arianna?"

Dawson jerked free and took another step. "None of your bus—"

"Everyone in this family is my business." Andrew sidestepped and blocked him again. "And I don't want her hurt."

That was code for what Dawson already knew in his heart to be true, not that he wanted to hear it from the young emperor here. "You mean I'm not good enough for her," he roared, infuriated. "You mean you don't want your poor relation of an ex-con half brother putting his filthy hands on a Warner princess."

Andrew, who'd never turned away from a fight, puffed out his chest and roared right back. "I mean she's vulnerable right now, and you've got some serious anger-management issues. You're mad at the world—"

"I'm mad at the Warners, yeah."

"—and I don't want to see her heart broken again. And if you cared anything about her at all, you'd know that already."

Wow.

There was the kick in the teeth he'd needed, the one that knocked all the angry bitterness right out of him. For now, anyway. Because he did know. Arianna wasn't for him on a good day, and his emotional reserves were so low right now that he was nothing but a walking disaster. He knew it. Too bad knowing it didn't make him want her any less. Ashamed suddenly, he ducked his head and turned away, hoping Andrew wouldn't see the turmoil that had to be simmering on his face.

He saw.

"Jesus," Andrew muttered, now looking at him as though he'd sprouted horns, a tail and purple feathers. "You're in love with her."

Whoa. The *L* word made Dawson's jaw drop, threatening to hit the floor with a clang. Talk about your ridiculous ideas. He wanted to snort with laughter, except that his mouth had gone bone-dry and he couldn't get his lungs to contract.

After way too long a pause, he managed a plausible denial.

"I don't believe in love."

"Neither did I," Andrew said. "You see where I'm at now."

Yeah, Dawson saw: Andrew had a wife and three boys and was apparently so happy with his domestic situation that seeing him and Viveca together was the rough equivalent of mainlining a five-pound bag of sugar.

Love. Please.

Ridiculous.

Except that Dawson's chest constricted another notch or two, threatening to lay him out flat on the cold black-and-white marble floor.

"You can't—" Dawson had to swallow back a huge-ass lump in his throat; where'd that come from? "—you can't fall in love with someone you just met."

Andrew stared at him. "I hate to tell you, my brother, but you can fall in love at first sight, and I'm speaking from personal experience."

"Bullshit," Dawson said, but there was no bite to the word, a fact that didn't seem to be lost on Andrew, who gave him a grim and, if he wasn't mistaken, pitying look. Dawson couldn't take it and folded like a house of cards staring down a hurricane. "Later for this." He tried to walk off again and got nowhere. Again.

Andrew called after him. "You've got to work on forgiveness, man. You can't hate the whole world and be the kind of man Arianna needs and deserves. You need to pull yourself together."

There was way too much truth in those three sentences—hell, in this whole conversation—and it scared him to death. And being scared only fed his anger, because God knew he'd spent far too much of his adult life being afraid of one thing or another.

"It's easy to talk about forgiveness when you've got everything life has to offer, isn't it, *my brother?*"

King Andrew was much too secure to let taunts from lesser relations make a dent in his armor. Shrugging it off, he spoke with calm conviction. "I didn't have everything until Viveca came along and I wanted to do better. So I could be with her."

Some of Dawson's anger deflated. There was no rebuttal for that, nor could he think of any way to deflect the growing list of things he and his half brother here had in common. "Well. Three cheers for you and Viveca."

Andrew's face twisted. "You don't make this easy, you know?"

"Things haven't been easy for me, so why should I take it easy on you?"

Andrew flushed; the light streaming in from the hallway's floor-to-ceiling windows highlighted his new color the way a spotlight highlights an actor on stage. To Dawson's surprise and intense discomfort, the brother pressed his lips together and looked…guilty. Almost ashamed.

And how the hell was Dawson supposed to deal with that?

"I'm sorry," Andrew told him.

"Save it."

Andrew, Mr. Arrogance himself, a man who'd probably never apologized for anything in his life, kept right on talking. "I should have tried harder to make peace with you. I should have tried harder to get Bishop to work things out with you. I should have tried harder to get you a better lawyer. We could have paid for it even after you refused—"

"I didn't want your charity then, and I don't want your pity now."

That, finally, shut Andrew up. Which was good, because Dawson didn't do emotional scenes, and he wasn't big on forgiveness just yet, even when a better man would've graciously granted it. His heart was too hard.

They faced off, and Andrew just had to push it.

"I'm sorry." Andrew's absolute determination to do the right thing and heal old wounds was so clear it might have been a tattoo etched across his forehead. "I'm sorry you lost years of your life for a crime you didn't commit. I'm sorry for every slight this family has given you. I'm—"

Dawson snorted. "Wow. Isn't your apology just the winning lotto ticket? Lucky me."

Andrew's expression hardened, which was what Dawson wanted. Even though he knew that made him a rotten SOB who'd just shot the peace dove with an AK-47, it was what his hard heart demanded. He had to hurt these people the way they'd hurt him.

Grimly satisfied, he enjoyed the utter rightness of his

world, at least until Andrew asked him the one question for which he'd never had an answer.

"I wonder, *Joshua,* do you ever get tired of being your own worst enemy?"

That stopped him dead, like a zap from a Taser.

He was his own worst enemy; he knew it. He'd spent countless excruciating sessions with his shrink down in Atlanta addressing this very issue. His pride kicked in, he got his panties in a bunch and he lashed out—always hurting himself way more than he hurt anyone else.

Case in point: When he was arrested those many years ago, the family stepped up to the plate. He hated to remember that now, but they did. Tried to contact him. Offered to hire a lawyer for him. And he, being young, hotheaded and, worst of all, stupid, had told them to go screw themselves. He'd nursed his anger at Bishop and the young king here and placed his faith in the justice system.

Yeah. That was a brilliant move.

What'd happened? Well, his pride had remained intact, that's what. Until his lame-ass court-appointed lawyer fell down on the job and bungled his way to a conviction.

Another case in point: right now. Andrew was his brother. Well…half, but still a brother. Dawson had claimed he wanted his rightful place in the family, and he'd always longed to fit in, to belong. Now here was a golden opportunity to usher in a new era in Warner family relations, and what was Dawson doing? Was he being mature and putting everything he'd learned during therapy into practice?

Hell, no.

He was doing the same old tired, knee-jerk, cut-off-his-nose-to-spite-his-face routine he'd always done.

What a smart boy he was. Genius, in fact. Did he think

this kind of winning behavior was going to shape him into a man who deserved a woman like Arianna?

Swallow the pride, Dawson. Turn over a new leaf.

Andrew was still glaring, still waiting.

And Dawson, suddenly, was tired of hating. So he gave an honest and heartfelt answer. "Yeah." He paused, clearing his craggy throat. "I'm pretty tired of being my own worst enemy. I'm, ah…I'm working on that. And I'm, ah…I appreciate…" Shit. You'd think he'd never spoken English before. He cleared his throat again. "I really appreciate…I mean…thanks," he finished lamely. "For the apology."

Andrew, looking gruff, gave a sharp nod and stuck out his hand.

Dawson took it.

They shook. He moved or maybe Andrew moved, and then without warning, they'd pulled each other in for a backslapping hug. It was familiar and strange at the same time, exactly what he'd needed even though he'd never known it. Some of the aching hurt that made its permanent home in his chest eased up, and he felt hot tears sting his eyes.

Blinking them back, he stepped away and dropped his head so Andrew wouldn't see. All his childhood, he'd looked up to Andrew, who'd always been the best and brightest, the most athletic and gifted, and tried to be as strong as him, as cool. That hadn't changed apparently, and he didn't want the brother to see him cry now.

So it was with utter astonishment that he raised his head and saw Andrew—Andrew!—swiping at wet eyes, his nostrils flaring. And then it got weirder.

"I missed you, man," Andrew told him.

Yeah, he'd missed Andrew, too, even with all the jealous rivalries they'd had over the years. But since he didn't do emotional stuff of any kind, other than his old pals Anger and Bitterness, it was far easier to lapse into sarcasm.

"Back off, all right? I think marriage has put you a little too in touch with your feminine side."

That broke them up. They laughed and it was all good, until Andrew threw him another curveball. "I know you're my brother. We'll do the DNA testing, just to dot all our *I*s and cross our *T*s and make it legal and official, but I know it. I accept it. Okay?"

Floored, Dawson stammered out a hoarse, "Yeah. Ah… thanks."

After nodding with unmistakable satisfaction, Andrew grabbed his face and planted a big one right on his cheek. Christ. The unexpected acknowledgment and affection meant so much to Dawson and were such head-spinning surprises that, for one terrible second, his lower lip quivered and he actually feared he'd start to bawl for the first time in about a hundred years.

Andrew—praise holy God—seemed to realize what was going on and took pity on him. He gave that same cheek a hard pat, just enough to clear Dawson's head, and then shoved him away.

They laughed again and hung their heads, shuffling their feet.

"Arianna, huh?" Andrew said.

Even the name did crazy shit to his insides. He shook his head, wondering what'd happened to him since he came back to Heather Hill, since he met that woman. Why couldn't he recognize himself anymore? "There's something about her, man."

"If you make her cry, I'm going to have to kill you. I don't care who the hell you are. Brother or no brother, I'll slice you up."

"Dude. I'm getting the picture."

"Especially since she's so vulnerable right now. I'm thinking this isn't the time for her to get into another relationship, but I know I don't get a vote."

"I understand. She mentioned a bad breakup but didn't give any details."

Andrew stilled, except for his eyes, which widened with surprise. Whoa. There was a story there, a big one, and Dawson wasn't sure he ever wanted to hear it.

"Ah," Andrew said, his gaze shifting away. "If she wants to get into it with you, she will. When she's ready."

Two days later, Arianna ran into Andrew in the driveway as he was throwing his overnight bag into the trunk of his car.

"Hey." His face was set in the kind of stern and concerned lines that told her he wanted to have a Very Important Talk. "You got a minute?"

She paused, taking longer than necessary to walk her bike across the gravel and lean it against one of the doors to the umpteen-car garage, while she gathered her thoughts.

Having just spent the last hour cranking her legs on the bike trail, she was hot and sweaty and not in the mood for any talk about Dawson/Joshua, which was probably what Andrew wanted. Why had she ridden her poor thighs to a burning cinder of quivering flesh? Because she'd been eating everything in sight and needed to expend some calories so she wouldn't end the week by weighing eight hundred pounds. Why was she eating everything in sight? Because she was obsessed with a certain not-good-for-her bad boy and needed to drown her sorrows in chocolate. It was either that or consume a bottle of champagne per night, and she really didn't think her inhibitions needed to be any lower where he was concerned, thanks.

And how could this situation get any worse?

With a suspicious Andrew on their tail, that's how.

Ever since Andrew saw them in the hall the other day, he'd been studying them with speculative eyes, and she could almost hear the wheels turning in his shrewd little mind, the connections being made. Andrew probably wanted to warn her against the resident bad boy, and she didn't even want the topic opened up for discussion. With her luck, Andrew would see her blush or something and realize she'd already slept with Dawson.

And wouldn't it be fun to hear Andrew's views on that?

Not.

"Ah," she began. "I probably should take a shower."

Andrew cracked a wry smile. "And by the time you're finished with your shower, I'll be on my way to the airport, and you won't have to listen to me."

"Oh." She widened her eyes and tried to channel the pure innocence of a newborn bunny. "Are you leaving?"

"You know we're leaving. This was only supposed to be a quick overnight trip until Bishop got sick. Nice try, though."

So much for that plan. Sighing, she planted her hands on her hips and prepared to be lectured, warned and browbeaten. "What is it?"

"You know what it is." His voice was so gentle she could almost believe he understood something about her situation. "What's up with you and Joshua?"

The obligatory denial rose right to her lips. "There's nothing—"

Andrew stopped her with a fly-shooing wave of his hand. "Let's pretend you've already given me that whole speech, and skip ahead to what I need to say. Before I miss my flight."

Crossing her hands over her chest, she glared and waited.

"You're into Joshua, and he's into you. Am I right?"

She twitched her shoulders in an irritable shrug.

"He's got a lot of baggage. A lot of bitterness. A lot of things he needs to work through."

"Golly gee," she interjected. "I hadn't noticed. Are you sure?"

Andrew ignored this, except for a narrow-eyed warning look. "But the thing is, he's a good guy. If you can crack through his hard shell. And…I think he probably needs you."

Wait—*what?*

Arianna pretended this information was only marginally interesting, when what she really wanted to do was grab Andrew by the collar and shake the whole story out of him. "Hold up. Did you just say…'a good guy'?"

His cheeks dimpled with poorly hidden amusement, probably because he knew he had her, the smug SOB. "I thought you said there was nothing—"

"Spit it out," she snarled.

"I want to tell you a little story that illustrates everything you need to know about Joshua."

Arianna was all ears.

"My—*our*—father was—" Andrew's jaw tightened and flexed "—well, I hate to speak ill of the dead, so let's just say he was a flawed human being." He paused. "A severely flawed, hateful and destructive human being. God rest his beloved soul."

Arianna snorted back a laugh.

"He considered himself a philanthropist, though, so he sent all of us, including Joshua and some of the other servants' kids, to nice private high schools. But he liked to lord it over us. Remind us that everything he had was either by the fruits of his labors or his good graces. Point out that we'd probably never amount to much and would certainly never achieve his godlike greatness. Are you getting the picture?"

"Oh, yeah."

"When Joshua got into Duke, dear old Dad would have paid for it, but Joshua had had enough of the second-class status. So he told the old man thanks but no thanks. Then he went on to get a scholarship and work two or three jobs—a full-time load—while being in school full-time and getting great grades. And Duke ain't cheap. You feel me?"

She nodded.

"Me? I happily took the Warner money and gave the old man the finger behind his back. Joshua? He wore his pride like a giant chip on his shoulder, but he's always been his own man. Even when he was eighteen."

Arianna filed all that away, to be examined later and added to what she already knew about Dawson/Joshua and his flawed but oh-so-fascinating character. "Why are you telling me this?"

Sighing, Andrew rubbed the back of his neck and stared off in the distance for a couple beats. Then he turned back, a smile in his eyes and a charming flush in his cheeks. "Because I was my own worst enemy once, too. And then I met Viveca. She made me want to do better. And I think you make Joshua want to do better."

Wow. With all that honesty and vulnerability on the table, she felt safer about opening up, just a little. "I can't fix him."

"Of course not. But you can inspire him."

"Being with him…it's a little scary. In a good way, I mean."

Andrew nodded with infinite understanding. "I get that."

"I'm afraid…he could really hurt me. If I let him."

"I get that, too."

"I'm not sure I'm ready, Andrew."

"I know." He hesitated. "You should tell him about Carter."

Okay, then. There was a limit to what she could talk about without her head exploding, and that was it. "I'll think about it. Now take your family home."

"You should listen to me. I'm always right."

"Yeah, yeah," she grumbled.

"And take care of Bishop."

"Will do."

With that, she went into the house for her shower, wondering if that bubbling feeling of hope in her chest meant that she was already on her way to giving Dawson another chance.

Chapter 11

"Another bite?" Arianna asked.

Bishop, who was sitting at the banquette in the massive kitchen, a napkin tied around his neck, with a spoon in one hand and a bowl of grits in front of him—salt and butter, no milk—glared.

Arianna locked her cheery smile in place, refusing to be cowed by either Bishop's attitude or the demoralizing process of helping him eat. Several little skills had been temporarily lost thanks to the TIA, and in addition to sessions with his occupational, speech and physical therapists, Bishop was practicing things like putting his socks on and buttoning his clothes. Members of the family helped.

Today's eating exercise had been, in her unprofessional opinion, an unmitigated disaster.

Bishop understood what the spoon was for and what he needed to do with it; he just couldn't make himself do it.

So far, he'd grasped the spoon upside down, backwards and sideways. Then, when they finally got the spoon in his hand properly gripped, he couldn't dip it into the bowl. When she helped him with the dip, he couldn't get it into his mouth. They'd been at it for about twenty minutes now, and although they'd jointly deposited grits on the table, his lap and the napkin on his chest, few of the grits had actually made it to his mouth.

It was possible that some other activity in the world, like, say, finding a needle in a haystack while blindfolded and wearing gloves, was more frustrating, but she doubted it.

They were both a little irritable, but she'd be damned if she'd show it. She was going to help Bishop back to one-hundred-percent health or die trying.

Or kill him while trying.

She smiled; he glared.

"Would you like me to feed you a couple bites?" she chirped. "You must be—"

Bishop pursed his lips and made a sound suspiciously like a raspberry.

"—really hungry."

He scooted to the edge of the banquette and started to get up, his frowning brows so low over his eyes it was a wonder he could see anything.

"You can't just quit. Are you quitting? Come on, now. Give it one more—"

Without a word, Bishop reached out, picked up the spoon and bent it in half.

Her jaw dropped. She was still gaping and Bishop was still glaring when the door swung open and Dawson strode in. The room's tension got to him pretty quickly, because by the third step he was slowing, and by the fifth he was looking like he wanted to divert into the wine cellar and hide there for the rest of the day. Still, he kept his game face on and Arianna awarded him silent points for trying.

"What's up, people?" he said in exactly the same falsely cheerful voice she'd been using for the last twenty minutes. "What'd I miss?"

Arianna ignored her heart's little skitter. Tried to ignore it. They hadn't seen much of each other for the last week or so, during which she'd resumed studying for the bar exam on top of helping Bishop, and she had the feeling he was giving her a wide berth in the huge house. Maybe he'd decided to stop pressuring her.

Why wasn't that possibility a relief?

She, meanwhile, was haunted by Andrew's words of advice.

Dawson looked good, and that didn't help. Today he wore a dark T-shirt and baggy shorts, a plain ensemble that he made unspeakably sexy. His gaze warmed at the sight of her, and something in the region of her chest (surely not her heart) tightened in response.

He seemed more peaceful lately, a little less angry, and that was also problematic. A harsh and moody Dawson was attractive enough, but a relaxed Dawson hovered right on the border of enchanting and devastating.

Taking the bent spoon, she held it up for Dawson to see. "Your father was just giving up on using utensils. Apparently he's decided to eat with his fingers for the rest of his life, so brace yourself. It's not pretty."

Scowling, Bishop ripped the napkin off his neck and threw it on the table. Then he jammed his hands on his hips in the biggest gesture of defiance she'd seen since that lone protestor faced down a tank in Tiananmen Square all those years ago.

"Is that true, Pop?"

Bishop said nothing, but his "screw you!" expression wavered for the first time.

"Hmm." Dawson reached out and put a hand on Bishop's neck, giving what looked like a reassuring squeeze. Arianna eyed that muscular arm sadly, thinking that Bishop would probably rip it out of its socket with his teeth, but both men surprised her.

Bishop took a deep breath and eased down, just a little.

And Dawson told her a story.

"Did I ever mention how I learned to ride a bike?" he asked her.

"No."

"The old man here, and Mama, gave me a bike for my seventh birthday. It was smooth, too. Blue, with those long handles and a banana seat—"

Arianna clapped a hand over her mouth. "*Please* don't tell me you had a banana seat."

"—and a crazy little horn that sounded like it belonged to an Edsel or something. *Ah-ooo-gah*. Like that." He sighed, lost in the memories. "Man, that was a sweet bike."

Bishop grunted, the edges of his mouth working at a grudging smile.

"Anyway," Dawson continued, "I wanted to put training wheels on it, because it was a big bike and looked like Mount Everest to me, you know, but this one—" he jerked his thumb at his father "—wouldn't hear of it."

Bishop held up his index finger and waggled it. "N-no wheels."

Dawson gave him a scathing sidelong glance. "Easy for you to say, old man. You already knew how to ride a bike, didn't you?" Bishop shrugged, somehow managing to make the gesture as smug as a smirk. "He threw me on that bike, ran along beside me, holding the seat to help me balance, and watched me fall onto the grass about two-point-four million times. And this was before kids wore helmets."

"Sad," Bishop said, and Arianna laughed.

"Hell yeah, it was sad. I was bruised and bloody, sweaty and stinky. I was cursing like a sailor, too, using all the bad words that Andrew taught me—"

Bishop shook his head. "Scooter. N-no good."

"—but by dinnertime, guess who knew how to ride a bike? Guess who was the proudest seven-year-old kid in the world?"

Bishop studied his son, the look in his eyes unreadable now. But then his chin quivered and his Adam's apple bobbed in a rough swallow. Dawson, meanwhile, never took his gaze off Arianna.

"And guess what Pop said when I scraped my knees and kicked the bike and said I'd just ride my Big Wheel instead."

Spellbound, Arianna shook her head.

"He quoted Napoleon to me: 'Victory belongs to the most persevering.' And so I kept getting back on that monster bike." Here it seemed to become significantly harder for Dawson to speak. Blinking furiously, he cleared his throat and took a minute to collect himself. "Napoleon has gotten me through some tough spots. He helped me keep my chin up when I was in prison, and he helped me build my real estate business." His voice dropped a notch, becoming huskier with a message Arianna knew was for her alone. "Anytime there's something I want—something I *really* want—I think about Napoleon and I work harder. And I wait until it's time."

Decoded message: he wanted her and wasn't giving up.

Oh, man.

Arianna stared at Dawson, slowly becoming unraveled. How was she supposed to stay away from this man when he was so endlessly fascinating and complicated?

The moment went on for too long and probably would have lasted longer, but Dawson came out of their mutual trance before she did. With a last shoulder squeeze and a clap on the back, he let Bishop go and headed back to the door from whence he'd come.

"So I don't think Pop's giving up on you," he said before he disappeared. "Why don't you see if he wants to try it again?"

They stared after him for a minute, and then Bishop turned that sharp-eyed gaze on her. She hunkered down, trying to get smaller, like a mouse in the grass, but she couldn't hide her burning face.

"Y-you like Josh-a?" Bishop asked.

"Yeah," she admitted. "I like Joshua."

Bishop nodded with clear satisfaction, resumed his place at the banquette and looked around for a new spoon. "Again try. No. Try...again."

"What've you got for me?" Dawson said into his cell phone a couple hours later.

He'd developed the habit of coming into the library after lunch, when it was usually quiet, and getting some work done at Arnetta's huge desk. Normally, he got a lot done.

Today, he felt as though someone had sucked all the brains out of his head and left soggy macaroni in their place.

Arianna. All Arianna, all the time.

Why couldn't he stop thinking about her?

Why wouldn't she take mercy on him and put him out of his misery?

"I'm emailing the letter right now." On the other end of the line, one of his real estate lawyers tapped a few buttons on his keyboard. "Give it a second."

"Great." Dawson scanned his email on his laptop, but no sign of it yet.

Bored, he leaned back in the chair, propped his legs on the desk and crossed one ankle over the other. It was a pretty day, he realized, not that he'd be able to enjoy it anytime soon what with all the calls he needed to make. On the other side of the French doors, the pool sparkled a deep and inviting blue. Maybe he could take a swim later. That would loosen up some of the tension in his lower back.

"Hi," Arianna said from the doorway. "Mind if I join you?"

Caught off guard, he swung his legs down, knocking a stack of papers to the floor in the process.

If Arianna noticed his clumsiness, she didn't let on. "I need a new place to study. I'm sick of the cottage." She breezed in carrying a massive pile of books, plopped down on the sofa and made herself at home there at the coffee table. "You don't mind, do you?"

"Do you see the email?" his lawyer asked in his ear.

Dawson clicked the phone off and tossed it onto the desk.

Deep in his rib cage, his heartbeat was going wild. This was the most progress he'd made with Arianna since their first night together, and being a cool cat was way beyond him at the moment.

Arianna seeking him out? Oh, yeah. This was progress.

"No. I don't mind."

"Good." Flashing a quick smile, she unzipped her backpack and slid out a laptop. "And I ordered a pizza. I get hungry when I study."

He eyed the grandfather clock. One-ten. "We just had lunch."

"Does ham and mushroom work for you? Thin crust?"

The grin began at one corner of his mouth and worked its way across; there was no stopping it. "Yeah. That works for me."

"And," she said, holding his gaze and tying his gut into knots that would take the rest of his life to undo, "I've decided to call you Joshua. Because that's who you are, no matter what you call yourself. Does that work for you?"

Dawson took a second to let this sink in.

Arianna wanted to share the room with him, eat pizza with him and call him by his real name. All this bountiful good fortune was on top of reaching detente with both his half brother and his adoptive father.

It wasn't outright victory yet, but it sure as hell wasn't going down in flames, either.

She wanted to call him Joshua.

And here was the funny thing: the more time he spent at Heather Hill, the more he felt like Joshua.

He nodded, using most of his energy to keep his butt firmly in the chair rather than climbing onto the desk and doing the Rocky dance on the balls of his feet with his fists in the air.

"Yeah," he said. "That works for me."

* * *

They developed a routine.

In the mornings, she helped Bishop with the fine motor skills, and Joshua drove him back and forth to his various therapies. When the men got back, they went for a swim, which was good for Bishop. After lunch, when Bishop grudgingly went to bed for a nap and Arnetta, more often than not, headed off for one of her charity committee meetings, Arianna and Joshua met alone in the library.

It was the best time of the day—except for the studying.

From her perch on the sofa, she could look up from her books and watch him pore over his paperwork, a furrow of concentration between his brows, his lips turned down in a frown. She could listen to the thrilling low murmur of his voice as he talked to his lawyers and employees, negotiating and making deals. She could enjoy the sudden surprise of his smile as he laughed at a joke and wonder what was so funny and if she could make him laugh as hard. She could wallow in the electric moments when he glanced up to catch her staring at him, and the want stretched between them, filling up the room.

He never touched her.

One afternoon during the third week, he threw his pen down, pushed away from the desk and stood. "I'm playing hooky."

Looking up from her torts notes, she frowned. "How are you going to make a million dollars today if you play hooky?"

"I'm not, but I need a break. So do you. Let's go."

"Where?"

"For a walk." Further surprising her, he held out his hand to help her up. "Come on."

She hesitated, utterly fixated on those long fingers with their blunt tips and trim nails. She knew those fingers, having sucked them into her mouth and felt them glide over every square millimeter of her body. That hand was a lethal weapon against which she had no defense.

Don't touch him, girl, warned her conscience in its annoying little voice. *You know you don't need to touch him.*

Good advice, but you know what? Screw you, conscience.

Reaching out, she slid her palm against his and let him pull her to her feet.

Mistake. Big mistake.

The electricity surged, so powerful it was a miracle she didn't see a shower of orange sparks. Her hand warmed, her arm tingled, her breath stopped. He stared unsmiling into her eyes, and she wondered what he saw when he watched her so intently and what about her attracted a man like this, because there were plenty of pretty women in the world, and she wasn't that interesting.

For one glorious second, his hand tightened around hers and he drifted closer, engaging her body in the magnetic pull from his, and she was so sure that this was it, the moment she'd dreaded and craved, the instant when he'd kiss her and get rid of all her uncertainty, once and for all, that her heart skittered and—

He let her go.

Her joyous heart hit the floor with a clanging clatter that felt like a metal trash can lid spinning to a stop on the street. She was so busy absorbing the sickening disappointment that it took her a minute to realize he'd walked to the door and was holding it open for her. His expression was a masterpiece of absolute serenity, like one of Monet's water lily paintings. If he'd felt anything a minute ago, he damn sure wasn't feeling it now.

"You ready?"

"Yeah." God, was her face as red as it felt? "Let's go."

Going for a walk, it turned out, was code for…going for a walk. Not saying much, they meandered past the pool and down the path by the cottage where she was staying and on down to the duck pond.

Nothing happened.

"So what are you going to do with Phoenix Legacies?" she asked when they were crossing the little bridge into the Japanese rock garden. "Have you decided what your project will be?"

"Not yet." He stared off in the distance, toward a quacking mallard that seemed determined to go a round or two with one of the black swans who thought it owned the section of the pond near the cattails. "I'm thinking I might work with the Innocence Program locally. They've got so many requests for help that they can't handle them all."

"Oh, wow," she began. "That's gre—"

Without comment, he took her hand.

One second they were walking, close enough to touch but not touching, their arms swinging together in an easy rhythm, and the next, her fingers were twined with his in that warm grip that made her insides soar. Yet he didn't make a big deal out of it, didn't bother even looking around to see if this was okay with her.

Luckily for him, it was so okay that she felt the heightening of all her senses and the subtle but insistent ache between her thighs. Hoping for a quick recovery that wouldn't clue him into her turmoil, she tried to pick up the threads of their conversation.

"—great. You could do so much good that way. You know what else would be good?"

"What's that?" he asked, now circling his thumb against her palm.

This was so not fair. How did he expect her to walk and talk when her knees were getting weaker by the second? "You could, ah, set up a network of employers willing to hire people just out of prison. Because so many—"

"Can't find jobs, yeah. I know. Hence my short but memorable career at the car wash."

"It's so hard for me to picture you working at a car wash. I'm surprised you weren't fired for insolence or something."

"I was headed in that direction. Fortunately, Governor Taylor rescued me before that happened. I was washing his car when he hired me." That thumb kneaded her palm in a rough caress, tapping into some hidden pressure point that turned her joints to warm pudding. "I finished up my shift that day, quit the car wash and never looked back."

"You made the most of your opportunity."

"I hope so."

That would have been the end of it. Still holding her hand and stroking her fingers, he angled off toward the gazebo, but she pulled up short. The muscles in his arm bunched up, registering his resistance, almost as though he knew where things were headed.

The whole time she'd known him, she'd thought of his experiences in the abstract, but now it was hitting her in all its ugliness, like a smack across the face with a dead fish.

The car wash was one thing. At least he'd been honestly employed. No problem. But...prison. *Prison.*

What horrors had he endured? What daily tortures, abuses and humiliations?

Of course he had anger-management issues—who wouldn't? Considering his wrongful conviction and excruciating family history, it was a miracle he hadn't gone to the nearest clock tower with a loaded rifle.

"Joshua."

She waited patiently until he met her gaze, his expression guarded.

"How did you survive?" she asked. "What saved you?"

"I don't know. I don't have some secret reserve of strength, if that's what you're getting at."

"Of course you do."

He shook his head in a firm and immovable no.

"What did you look forward to? What kept you hanging on? Clearing your name? Getting revenge against your family?"

"Nothing like that. The only thing I can tell you is that I figured that things could only get better, and if I hung on long enough, the good days, when they finally came, would be spectacular. It's only fair, right?"

"And have they? Been spectacular?"

He laughed. "Well, every day when I can get up when I want to and go outside when I feel like it is a good day."

"But what about *spectacular?*" she persisted.

His smile faded. In no particular hurry, he looked down at her hand and massaged it with both of his, a bone-deep caress that seemed to have nothing to do with her hand and everything to do with the emotions that darkened his face.

And then, at last, he kissed her palm, curled her fingers in to hold the kiss and flicked that turbulent gaze up to her eyes. He stared at her so hard and for so long that she wondered if anyone had ever seen her before—if anyone had ever looked. Then the confession came, and it was reluctant, as though he resented having to tell her something so intimate and yet couldn't wrestle the words into submission.

"Spectacular didn't start until I met you."

That was when she came to the fork in her road and faced down the decision she'd been putting off. On the one hand, she could play it safe and turn away from this man. Hell, she could head to New York and finish the exam prep there, spending a little extra time with her brother, Sandro. The bar was in a couple of days, and it wasn't like she was really needed here anyway, so why not pack up her study guides, hop the next plane and send Joshua a text: CU L8R.

Nice clean break, problem solved.

Except that she'd spend the rest of her life—and she was young, so she had a good long while to suffer—thinking about what they'd already shared and what they might still share, if she had the guts to let go of her fears, have some faith and give him another chance.

Standing there under bright blue skies on a day full of possibilities, staring into his brown eyes, getting lost in him, she took the plunge.

"I'm crazy about you, Joshua—"

He took a sharp breath.

"—you know that, don't you?"

"I didn't know."

Regret came knocking on her door, looking for an opening. "I shouldn't have told you that."

"It's okay," he said quickly.

"Really?" She raised an eyebrow, pretty sure she'd just

performed the emotional equivalent of leaping onto the subway tracks just ahead of the five o'clock train. "And how does it make you feel?"

He thought hard, the corners of his eyes crinkling with one of those internal smiles he did so well. "Happy. Scared."

"Yeah? Which one do you feel the most?"

This time there was no hesitation. "Happy."

Now was the time for him to take some of the pressure off, to wrench her into his arms and kiss her until her lips swelled and fell off. But he held back, tension vibrating through him, and she figured he wanted to put any decisions about where they went from here solely into her lap because he was done pressuring her. Too bad she didn't know what to do other than delay what looked like the inevitable.

"We should talk about this some more when I get back from New York, don't you think?"

"Hell, yeah," he said. "I think."

"Good."

A delicious moment passed as they stared into each other's faces.

Then she tugged his hand and they resumed their walk.

"Did something, ah, happen, Sandro?"

Arianna poked her head into her brother's bedroom, praying she wasn't taking her life into her hands by coming in here and asking. To her dismay, she saw an overnight bag open on the bed; that couldn't be good. After finishing up the second day of the bar exam in New York City yesterday, she'd made the trip out here to Sag Harbor and her parents' estate, where Sandro lived now. They'd intended to spend the weekend together eating lobster, walking on the beach and catching up, but it looked like those plans were about to go up in smoke.

"I heard you talking on the phone," she continued.

Talking was a bit of an understatement. From her room down the hall, where she'd been thinking about getting up to start her day, she'd heard Sandro yelling the way she imagined he used to yell at his men when they were under fire in Afghanistan. Since she hadn't heard gunshots and didn't imagine he'd unleashed that fearsome temper on the housekeeper for, say, not dusting under the bed, she figured the ringing phone she'd heard a few minutes ago had brought some unpleasant news.

"Yeah." He'd been over at the dresser, finding underwear and socks, but now he swung around and walked to the bed, his back yardstick straight and his bearing as rigid and square-shouldered as if he'd taken a momentary break from the military parade he'd been marching in. "Your nephew got himself kicked out of summer camp. Again. He designed a virus that shut down the computer lab. Nice, huh? I need to go fetch him and listen to the list of his misdeeds."

"Oh, no." Deciding to risk it, Arianna came all the way into the room and sat on the edge of the bed, a little too close to the precise line of perfectly folded clothes he'd arranged, judging from the dark glance he threw her. "Sorry," she said, scooching back and taking care not to unduly wrinkle the gray duvet in the process. *"Sorry."*

Sandro was, in her opinion, just a couple of notches away from a full-blown and intransigent case of obsessive-compulsive disorder. Take this room, for example: austere enough to qualify as a monastery, with a couple of pieces of boxy modern furniture, a flat-screen TV and not a single plant, photo, lost slipper or particle of dust to warm the place up or indicate that a human being lived here. His years in the military had not helped iron out the neatness issue, no question, but she wasn't going to point that out to him just now. One major problem at a time was all she could handle, especially when her brain was fried from two days of the bar exam.

"So what are you going to do with him now?" she asked.

"Military camp."

"What?" If she'd wanted to think of the worst possible answers to her twelve-year-old nephew's wayward behavior, military camp would be in the top three. "He doesn't need another camp. He needs to spend time with you and adjust to you being back home. And his mother walking out."

Sandro, who'd leaned over and begun rolling up his clothes for meticulous insertion into the overnight bag, paused. His head slowly came up and he hit her with a blast of his icy displeasure: lowered brows, thinned lips, the brown flash of anger in his eyes.

Arianna had to fight not to shrink inside her skin, and she was a grown woman. She could just imagine what this fearsome routine did to Sandro's troubled boy.

"And how many children do you have?" Sandro asked.

"None," she admitted.

"Then why are you talking?"

"Sandro."

Throwing caution to the wind, she gripped his wrist with the idea of comforting him and showing him that they both wanted the best thing for the boy. Instead, she got a handful of flesh as unyielding as iron, wound up so tight it was a wonder he could move and breathe at all.

"You can't send him away forever. One of these days, you and he will have to deal with each other and put your family back together." *Without Samantha,* the witch who'd walked out because she couldn't handle being a military wife, but Arianna didn't add that.

Sandro yanked his arm free. "What he needs," he said, zipping his bag closed and picking it up, "is less spoiling and hand-holding, and more discipline."

With that, he walked out, taking all the air in the room with him.

"Wow." Flopping over backward on the bed, Arianna stared at the ceiling. "That went well."

Emptiness hit her in a wave. The house rang with silence, and her thoughts, as they always did, swung back around to Joshua. What was he doing now? What would he say about Sandro and son? Would he tell her not to worry? Would he have suggestions on how to deal with them?

Did he miss her the way she missed him?

Before she could talk herself out of it, she fished the cell phone out of her robe pocket and called him. They'd texted each other since she'd been gone, but that wasn't the same.

"Hey," he answered halfway through the first ring. "I was hoping you'd call."

"Hey." It was really crazy the way the sound of his voice made her feel better. "How are you?"

"The question is, how are you? Did you get some sleep?"

Not really. Because she'd been thinking of him. "Yep."

"You don't sound so good. What's wrong?"

Did he know her that well, or did she sound that bad? Suddenly she felt terrible for having bothered him at all.

He was probably in the middle of some million-dollar deal and didn't need to hold her hand. And she didn't need to depend on him when his track record was so sketchy. "Oh, I'm fine. It's just, you know, Sandro's having a little trouble with his son. No big deal. I'll let you get back to work. Bishop okay today?"

"He's fine, but—"

"You have a good day, okay?" *I miss you. God, I wish you were here.*

"Arianna—"

"Bye."

Chapter 12

Alone with her yammering thoughts, Arianna puttered around the house for a while. After weeks of intense studying and worrying about both the bar exam and Bishop, it was strange to think that the exam was behind her (what was she supposed to do with her time now, eh?) and Bishop was on the road to recovery. She still planned to spend the rest of the summer at Heather Hill, but what about Sandro and son? Who'd look after them and help them nurture their relationship? And what about a job—shouldn't she find one somewhere and start her career as a lawyer?

And what about Joshua? They'd agreed to discuss their relationship when she got back to Columbus, and that deadline was looming, but what would they say? Where would they go from here? Plus, the whole Carter thing was still outstanding, and she needed to tell him about that.

She felt a little lost, a little forlorn.

So when the swirling worries overcame her, she went for a long walk on the beach and focused only on the gulls flapping overhead and the sand squishing between her toes. That helped. Then she showered and went out to the terrace to lounge, watch the waves and read her book, whereupon she fell into a coma and slept for three hours. That really helped.

She'd just wandered back into the kitchen and poured herself some chardonnay—the housekeeper had very kindly left clam chowder and some other goodies for her in the fridge, she saw—when the doorbell rang and she heard the low murmur of voices. Curious, she wandered down the long hall and into the entry, sipping her wine as she went.

When she rounded the last corner, she got the surprise of her life.

Joshua stood there next to the wide-eyed housekeeper, who seemed torn somewhere between vague alarm and feminine appreciation. The second he saw Arianna, his searching gaze latched on to her face and held.

Arianna froze.

"Ah, Arianna," the housekeeper said, as though the most normal thing in the world was for a dreadlocked, tattooed and muscle-bound man to show up unannounced on their private estate and ask for Arianna, "you have a visitor."

Arianna was too shocked to speak.

"Should I serve some iced tea?" the housekeeper continued.

Arianna still couldn't speak.

"I'm good," Joshua said, his eyes still on Arianna.

"Well, if everything's okay here, I'll just go back to

the laundry room," the housekeeper said, now looking bemused, and left.

"Hi." A hint of a smile crinkled the edges of Joshua's eyes.

Arianna's voice finally reappeared. "What are you doing here?"

"I was…in the neighborhood?" he tried.

Arianna shook her head.

"No?" Joshua thought for a second and tried another tactic. "I was in the city and just stopped over for a—"

She shook her head again.

He quit with the excuses. "Could you make this easy for me, maybe?"

"No. Sorry."

He stared at her, running his hand over the back of his neck. The poor lighting and early evening shadows couldn't hide the flush as it crept over his cheeks. "I was worried about you. I…missed you."

Arianna blinked, trying to think of a way that his sudden appearance to check on her wasn't a huge deal. "Joshua, traffic on and off the island is horrible during the summer. You can't just—"

"Helicopter," he informed her.

Helicopter.

Her head spun with this information. Joshua had dropped whatever he was doing to hop a plane, and then a helicopter, to come out to the Hamptons and see her. Because he was worried about her and missed her.

And she was utterly, hopelessly and desperately in love with this man.

"That's quite a gesture." There was more, but she didn't say it. God knew what she'd confess right now if she kept talking.

"You're quite a woman."

Yeah, she thought. It was definitely love. Like she'd never known it.

"So." Looking a little awkward, he shifted on the balls of his feet and shoved his hands in his pockets. "Are you going to kick me out?"

"Oh, no." Something unstuck within her, and she smiled, unable to keep the crazy joy locked up inside. "I think we should go for a swim. You can borrow Sandro's trunks."

The pool was a hidden masterpiece of sparkling blue, surrounded on three sides by swaying masses of black-eyed Susans, hostas, grasses and, by the smell of it, heather. The long fourth side gave the illusion of disappearing into the roaring navy surf in the distance and, beyond that, the horizon. If he wasn't so excited to be with Arianna, his belly so tied up in delicious knots of hope and desire, he'd have taken a moment to be stunned by this secluded heaven on earth here in the Hamptons.

She was already there, swimming at the far end.

"Hey." Ignoring his stomach's crazy flip, he began the long walk to where she paddled, treading water. "You started without me."

Seeing him, she stretched out and moved in his direction, her arms circling in an easy doggy paddle that didn't splash the water. "You can swim, right?"

"Don't worry." Kicking off his flip-flops, he took off his shirt and glasses, tossed his towel on a chair and dipped a toe. "I've got gills."

She laughed, and the sound was a seductive dance across his skin and up and down his spine, so thrilling he couldn't stop a shiver. "Come on in."

He dove, slicing through the bathwater warmth and heading straight for her. Without his glasses, things were a little blurry, but he could see her beautiful face, smiling as she approached, and the wet tail of her black hair as it swirled around her shoulders.

She reached for him and, hell, that was clear permission to reach for her, but just as his hand skimmed her shoulder, she laughed and flipped, emerging several feet away. Now on her back, she swept one arm overhead and then floated, drifting, and that was when he saw them.

Nipples. Two of them. Sticking out of the water.

Holy shit.

Struck stupid, he gaped, his mouth flapping as though hinged. "Arianna," he said finally, his voice strangled, "what happened to your bathing suit?"

With a wicked laugh, she stroked by, still out of touching range, flipped again and reappeared on her stomach, her round ass sticking out of the water behind her head. His eyes bulged so hard he'd swear he could feel their connective tissue stretching and tearing. His glasses! Why hadn't he worn his glasses?

"I didn't mean to offend you," she said. "I'm happy to wear something. Would that make you feel better?"

"No," he barked. "That would *not* make me feel better."

"Whatever makes you happy."

"This is making me pretty happy right now, I gotta tell you. Where's the housekeeper?"

"I gave her the night off."

Gave her the night off.

Joshua gaped, unable to believe his massive good fortune at being alone on this estate with a naked and apparently willing Arianna. This couldn't be happening. Or, if it was happening, there was a speeding meteor heading in his direction and he had mere seconds to live.

At least he'd die happy, though.

She came closer, treading water now, her grin mischievous and wry. As he watched—and, yeah, he was staring, and it never occurred to him to pretend he wasn't—she swirled those arms again. While he struggled not to drown, what with all his blood being diverted away from his kicking legs and straight to his rock-hard penis, she rose out of the water just enough for her breasts to bob to the surface and linger there, walnut-tipped and plump, the water sliding over them with gentle lapping sounds.

He swore. "On second thought, if you're just planning to torture me, then maybe you should wear, I don't know, a wet suit or something."

"Poor Joshua." Sultry as a water nymph, she reached out and, her actions hidden by the water, scraped her nails low over his belly. He groaned. "Do you want to touch me?"

"Yeah," he said hoarsely.

"How much?"

Licking his lips and swallowing convulsively, he tried to be cool, but that ship had already sailed. "I'm shaking with it." He hesitated, but hey, why not be honest? "I'm dying with it."

"Then come here."

They flowed together, and the second she came within reach, she wrapped those silky limbs around him, clinging like a drowning victim. Her mouth was already open, her tongue surging for his, and they nipped, licked and sucked their way to a pulsing rhythm that matched the thrust of their hips. She tasted so freaking perfect, God, and the flexing globes of her bare ass felt just right in his hands. Losing control by the mile, he ground her against him, searching for that one right spot between her legs, and when he found it, her sharp cry was his sweet reward.

One ounce of sense remained, and he hurried to use it before it shriveled up and died. "Yes or no, Arianna?"

"Yes," she said against his lips. "It's always yes with you. Pool house."

He'd already seen it at the far end of the pool. Lit and welcoming, it had open French doors and sheer white panels that fluttered at all the windows. "Pool house. Great."

He let her go, which was hard. She swam to the steps and climbed out, the water streaming down her body in glittering ribbons. Staring to his heart's content, he watched and noted the contraction of every toned muscle as she walked. She was glorious—all sleek curves and gleaming skin, her ass a delicious heart topped with two deep dimples. Humbled, he filed this moment away because he knew nothing like it would ever come again.

Reaching a chaise, she turned, giving him the full-frontal view of gently bouncing breasts and that black triangle between her legs. She didn't bother with a towel. Instead, she grabbed a big scarf-type thing—sarong, wasn't it?—wrapped it around her body and tied it at the neck. Only, the sarong was sheer and white and she was soaking wet. The mind-blowing result was a tantalizing view of everything through a tissue-thin layer that clung to her skin. Jutting nipples and the heavy, round curves of her breasts…slightly rounded belly…that sexy mound at the top of legs…the legs…

Light-headed with lust now, far beyond any sexual experience he'd ever had, and he'd had plenty, he opened his mouth and struggled to put it into words, to tell her—

"Arianna."

She paused and waited.

It was all there on the tip of his tongue, too much for him to ever possibly say. He floundered and then managed to get part of it out: "Thank you for giving me another chance."

She stared at him for long seconds, almost like she saw everything he couldn't say and understood it better than he'd ever guess. And then, just when the moment became too significant, too intense, too much, she smiled gently and it was okay. Every one of his fears—of betrayal and abandonment, of never belonging, never being judged worthy or loved—eased back to a manageable level.

What could be so wrong, with a smile like that in the world?

What could happen?

Couldn't his life, just this once, turn out okay?

Yeah, came the answer. *With her, it could.*

Arianna held out her hand. "You can thank me in the pool house."

After a quick stop in the bathroom for a couple of fluffy towels, they headed straight for the small bedroom. Just as the complete darkness registered with his overheated brain and he was thinking of lodging a protest, she clicked on a lamp over on the dresser. The room came into focus: lots of expensive country-style furniture centered on a four-poster bed.

And the only thing he really needed to see, Arianna—the best thing that ever had, or possibly could, happen to him. She stared into his face with utter focus, the way she'd done that first night, and there was a glow in her expression, an amazing half smile that was his reward for the struggles he'd had up until now. If someone showed up to ask him if it'd been worth it, his "yes" would come without hesitation.

Spectacular. Yeah.

Every moment with her was spectacular, and this was off the charts.

They didn't talk. There was too much to say.

First things first. She was wet, and he wouldn't be doing his job if he let her get cold. So he concentrated on peeling that sheer nothing up her thighs, over that black triangle, past the wide curves of her sweet hips and amazing breasts, and off, to the floor. A certain amount of regret hit him; he'd miss that tantalizing view of her body partially hidden from him.

This was better, though.

Taking the towel, he ran it over her head and gently squeezed her hair. Back, shoulders and arms came next, slow and easy, because they had all night, he'd waited a long time for this and if he couldn't get his words to work, he sure as hell could touch her right. The sounds she made told him he was headed in the right direction. Jesus. He remembered those sounds. Low, humming croons of pleasure vibrated in her throat, as though anything he did to her was perfect and she'd be satisfied with just this.

He, on the other hand, wouldn't be satisfied until her sounds filled up the house. So he trailed that towel down her belly, skimming it with a light touch, until he reached that lovely cleft between her legs. There, he stroked.

Bingo. A sharp cry rose up as though he'd surprised her. Nice. He liked that. What if he stroked again, harder? A moan this time, with the added bonus of her eyes widening and clouding over at the same time. It drove him wild the way she stared and stared at him, like he was the important one between the two of them, as though she didn't want to miss any of his reactions when he was so fascinated by all of hers.

The towel had served its purpose, and he needed his hands on her. Tossing it aside, he cupped that amazing face and kissed her slowly, gently, keeping it to a tiny taste even when she wanted more and her frustrated tension shivered under his hands.

Nice and easy tonight. That was the name of the game.

Leaving that sweet mouth with a little reluctance, yeah, he cupped a breast in each hand, squeezed them together, stuck his tongue out and licked down her neck, heading for those pointed nipples. He circled each one with his tongue, getting no closer than her areolae—damn, they were darker now, a deep blackberry that looked unbelievably sweet—aaannnd no. Not yet, sweetheart. She'd begun to writhe, to try to bring his head closer by digging the tips of her short little nails into his nape, but he was pretty sure she could go hotter and melt down a little more.

That would be fun.

What if he worked his way up the other side of her neck, using his whole mouth this time, licking and sucking his way to her lips? Ah, yeah. She liked that. Gasping with a whole lot more desperation than she'd shown a minute ago, her lungs heaving for air under his hands, she opened for him, and he kissed her a little harder this time, a little deeper.

Those sounds of hers changed. They broke down a little, became a little more animalistic and raw. Cool. Except that this wasn't a clinical procedure for him, and he couldn't pour everything into her without taking a little bit for himself. He was way too hard for that, his blood too hot and his skin too tight.

So he pressed those breasts together, plumping them up even more, scraped his tongue across each nipple one time, just to refamiliarize himself with her texture, which was pebbly and velvety, like the sweetest summer raspberry, and sucked. Hard.

This time her cry was shocked, strangled, and her knees went soft as she arched to give him more access. That was when he slammed headfirst into the limits of his control.

Bed. Now.

Popping that nipple out of his mouth and taking just a quick second to appreciate the way her breast stretched and jiggled back into place, reforming those three perfect circles—nipple, areola, breast—he grabbed her up in his arms, swung her around to the bed and laid her down.

Arianna, who seemed to have been born with an extra female gene that made him pant, want and ache more than he'd ever done in his life, arched for him, arms high overhead, back curved, belly softly rounded, juicy thighs parted just enough to reveal how ready she was and how she glistened for him.

His foolish hopes of playing Iron Man of Steel and stretching her pleasure out forever gave their final gasp and died. Yeah, he was a punk. Quick Draw McGraw, that was him. He'd be lucky if he lasted two seconds, but screw it. Now. He needed to be inside her NOW.

Too bad his limbs no longer worked. Jerking and kicking his way out of his trunks, he lunged for the condoms she'd cleverly left on the nightstand. Good girl. But then she shifted to her side, rested her face on her hand and gave him a smile that was all glittery eyes and sultry promise, and his spasming heart lurched its way that much closer to full cardiac arrest.

"It's not time for that yet," she told him.

"But—"

With a laugh, she crept on all fours to the edge of the bed, cupped and squeezed his balls and took him deep into the hot pulsing slickness of her mouth.

Oh, the irony.

Now *his* lungs heaved, desperate for just one molecule of air. Now *his* sharp gasps bounced off the walls. Now *he* grabbed *her* head to hold her close, his fingers buried in the hair at her nape, determined to keep her there until the pleasure made him collapse and die.

She didn't wait to hear his protestations about being on the razor's edge and this being a terrible idea if she wanted him to last for the actual lovemaking. She didn't seem to care that the sight of her flexing ass stuck in the air was making him unravel. She didn't ask if her throaty hums intensified his sensations beyond all human endurance.

She just kept going, flicking and sucking his sensitive head, squeezing his balls and then, with no warning, plunging him deep into her throat with a bob of her head.

It was so freaking good…she was so amazing. He'd never… Man, he was going to come—

"*Stop,* Arianna."

Yeah, he was undone. Unmanned, unraveled and unworthy. Wrenching her away—and she seemed very reluctant to go, by the way—he reached for those condoms again and eyed her with new respect, his Arianna. She had a trick or two waiting for him, and he was going to grow old and then die a happy man discovering them all.

Ready at last, he climbed over her and grabbed her hips to flatten her on her back. The look on her face had been unvarnished female smugness, but now, at the crucial moment, she cocked her hips and stared up at him again. God, she was intense. Sweat dampened her face and beaded down between her breasts, and he intended to lick it off in a minute and then make her sweatier.

For now, he just wanted to pause and enjoy.

His woman. This amazing creature was his. And, whether she knew it or not, after tonight, she always would be. She'd said she was crazy about him, so maybe she knew it. God knew he was already so far around the bend over her, he'd never come back.

He tried to smile, she tried to smile back, but they both failed spectacularly.

"I missed you," he told her.

"I missed you, too," she answered.

Then he hooked one of his elbows under one of her knees, and spreading her wide, plunged as deep inside her as he could go.

Ecstasy gestured a hand at him, inviting him closer, and thrusting his hips, he went. A second thrust made her come. Amidst all the sweet sucking pleasure of her inner muscles as they convulsed around him, another feeling washed over him. It was a deep, relieved breath, a bottomless peace and the kind of belonging he'd never thought he'd find.

Deep inside his head, a voice spoke for the first time ever.

I'm home.

Later, after they'd made love two more times and lay twined together in a drowsing tangle of arms and legs, she stroked the side of his neck. "I've been meaning to ask about your tattoo."

"It's an Adinkra peace symbol. From the darkest days of my wild past."

"Hmm." She traced the shape, which was an intricate black tic-tac-toe board with rounded ends. "No offense, but—*peace?* You? Didn't they have a bitter, screw-the-world tattoo available that day? Maybe an exploding peace dove or something?"

"Funny. My anger-management issues are why I got the thing. It's supposed to remind me to search for peace."

She raised her head just long enough to shoot him a dubious look, brows arched. "How's that working for you?"

"It's aspirational," he said. "Let's leave it at that, okay?"

"If you say so," she said, grinning and snuggling down again.

His turn for a question. "Where should we live?"

Against his chest, he felt the apple of her cheek swell with a smile. "Are we going to live together?"

"Yes."

"What are our choices?"

"Anywhere with a bed."

She laughed, the sound low and rusty, and it was the warmth his soul needed. "Can you be more specific?"

"I can work anywhere, Ari. What would you like?"

"Would I be pushing my luck if I suggested the possibility of us thinking about the outside chance of us living in Columbus, so we can be near Heather Hill?"

"Yes," he said flatly, rolling his eyes, but he'd suspected she'd say that. "You just took the New York bar, remember?"

"Well, yeah. I can take the Ohio one, too."

"Another bar exam. Fun."

"Can we talk about it?"

"I'm in a pretty good mood tonight, so, yeah, we can talk about it."

"Good."

They'd talk about other stuff, too, but he wasn't planning to mention that now. He didn't want to scare her off, not when her trust in him was still fragile and new.

But he'd been doing a lot of thinking. About the emotional wounds he was still working through and the progress he'd made. About the things he'd expected from his life and the unexpected turns it'd taken since he met Arianna.

He'd learned something funny: his heart could heal. It didn't have to be so hard. Old relationships with his family could be renewed and strengthened, and this new relationship with Arianna could be nurtured until it grew into the strongest redwood sequoia, able to withstand just about anything life threw at it.

As far as he was concerned, there was a big word lurking in their future. It didn't scare him shitless, much to his surprise, and he didn't want to run screaming in the other direction. He wanted to sprint for it and catch it in his hands.

Marriage.

With this one woman, he could feel at home and trust that things really were what they seemed. He could be himself with her, because she saw and understood him the way he did her. They fit together, and she awakened parts of him that'd been presumed dead for years. With her in his life, it wasn't such a stretch to imagine a happiness that would last past tomorrow and the next day, nor did it strain his brain too much to imagine—he did a small mental gulp—children. They made a good team, the two of them. And he'd make sure that their kids never knew the kind of turmoil he'd experienced growing up.

Her breathing evened out and she snuggled closer in her sleep, finding the exact right spot against his side. Deep inside him, something swelled to the size of a hot-air balloon, threatening to burst free and shower little bits of him all around the room.

In his entire life, he'd never felt anything this fiercely, not even bitterness.

There in the darkness, with the slow rise and fall of

her ribs beneath his fingers, he made two promises to himself.

One: he was going to marry this amazing woman.

Two: he'd never voluntarily spend another night without her warm and snug in his arms, exactly like this.

Chapter 13

They returned to Heather Hill the next day, where they resumed their routine, with one delicious modification: he spent his nights with her at the cottage. This morning, as he headed up the hall toward the library, where he'd made plans to meet Arianna after he showered and changed up in his room, Joshua gave his mental to-do list a silent run-through. First thing on the list: checking in with the old man to see how he was doing so far, and if he'd managed to feed himself any grits off that spoon today. And then—and this was the crazy part, but what the hell—he wanted to tell Pop about his relationship with Ari. They'd been back for a week, and it was—

The sound of an angry voice nearby hit his ears, a note as discordant on this lush summer morning as hip-hop dancers in the middle of *Swan Lake*.

He froze, that ugly prickle of foreboding crawling up his spine the way it used to do when he was in the pen.

Another burst of ugly helped him zero in on the sound: the library, dead ahead.

An energy boost kicked in, especially when a woman's sharp voice climbed over a man's urgent rumble. *Arianna.* A fanged creature sprang to life inside him and propelled him the last several feet. He didn't know what the hell was going on, but his role was clear as the glasses on his nose. If someone was giving his woman shit, it was time for him to take someone off at the knees. Period.

"I don't understand what you're doing," Arianna cried on the other side of the door. "It's all settled—"

"Not to me, it's not." The man's desperation was palpable, like black exhaust fumes heavy in the air. "I still love you. We can make it work. I know we can."

That was when the ugly inside Joshua got fierce, threatening to gnaw its way through his flesh until there was nothing left except a few scraps of skin. The possessive creature was still there, too, demanding that he sort everything else out later, for sure, but protect his woman now.

NOW.

Hot and icy at the same time, a roiling combination of fury that should be locked in a subterranean cave away from people, he banged through the door and into the library.

He didn't like what he saw, but then he'd known he wouldn't.

Arianna wheeled around, her already stricken face turning distraught at the sight of him. Guilty color in her cheeks and a whole lot of *let me explain* in her eyes. A terrible rawness in her voice as she reached out a hand to him.

"Joshua..."

Next to her was the sight that really did him in and

kicked the air right out of his gut. The dude, a Wellington Bentley Smithson IV type, with his polo shirt, khakis and loafers, stood there looking princely and as possessive as Joshua felt.

A quick glance took in the guy's wavy black hair, arrogant chin and to-the-manor-born entitlement, and told Joshua everything he needed to know. Dude here hadn't grown up in the caretaker's cottage with his face pressed up against the window of the big house. Dude here hadn't wondered about his place in the world or why his real daddy denied him and his adoptive father hadn't wanted him. Dude here had never spent time behind prison bars, wrongfully or otherwise.

Bottom line? Dude here, who was as different from Joshua as a brick was from a bar of gold bullion, was exactly the kind of man who belonged with a princess like Arianna. Exactly the kind of man Joshua could never be.

For this reason, if nothing else, Joshua wanted to scrape the guy's face off his skull with a teaspoon.

"Joshua," Arianna said again, agonized, but he ignored her for now because he only had eyes for the guy.

"Who the hell are you?" he demanded, fully aware that the low menace in his voice was like the rasp of a blade against a sharpening stone.

"Arianna's husband," the guy said.

The *H* word was still reverberating in Joshua's head, clanging around like bowling balls in a metal trash can, when Arianna sprang into action. "Ex-husband," she told Joshua, barely meeting his eyes. "He's my *ex*—"

"Barely," said the guy. "And I want to change that—"

"We've been separated for eighteen months." Now Arianna divided her wild-eyed glances between the two of them, gesturing with her arms for emphasis. "We tried counseling and it didn't work. We tried a trial separation and that didn't work, either. The divorce was final at the beginning of the summer. That's that—"

"You were married to this guy?" Joshua questioned, staring at the woman who'd meant so much to him and was only, he now realized, the latest in a long line of people in his life who weren't what they'd seemed. Another pretender, another betrayer. He should've known. Should've freaking known. "Did you think you should mention that?"

To her credit, pretty little lying Arianna didn't dissolve into a fit of tears. Blinking furiously to hold back the wetness in her eyes, she kept her chin up and her voice firm. Well, he'd known she was strong, hadn't he? That much about her, at least, was the truth.

"My marriage is over," she said flatly. "I should have told you, yeah, but it has nothing to do with us, and what happened before I met you is really none of your business."

He almost laughed, it was all so ridiculous—especially the pulsating wreckage of what had been his heart. What had the Tin Man said in *The Wizard of Oz?* Now I know I have a heart because it's breaking, or some shit like that? Yeah. That worked for him.

"Really, Ari? Is that how we're playing it now?" To his fierce satisfaction, her lower lip quivered and a single tear traced a path down her beautiful face. It felt good, her pain. It felt nice to dish her up a millionth of the agony she'd just served him on a silver platter. But then another tear fell and it hurt too much to look at her, so he turned to the guy. "Do you have a name, Mr. Ex-Husband?"

The man stared, his attention swinging between Arianna and Joshua. Apparently he was getting the picture in full high-def, because his face kept darkening by the second. Finally he zeroed in on Joshua, and his jaw all but solidified to concrete. "Carter Smith," he said, low. "And you are…?"

This time a burst of laughter did escape from Joshua's throat, and it was so bitter it twisted and stretched his lips like a gargoyle's. "Well, Carter, you can take your pick. You can either call me Joshua Bishop or, depending on your mood, you can call me Dawson Reynolds. It's up to you."

He pivoted, keeping Arianna in his sights, because God knew he had to keep an eye on her lest she try another bait-and-switch routine on him when he least expected it. The raw pain in his chest drove him on, pushing him to hurt her more, harder.

"As for you, sweet little Arianna, don't you think it's a little—what's the word?—hypocritical? Ironic? I like *hypocritical*, so I think I'll go with that. Don't you think it's a little hypocritical for you to make such a big deal about my real name, when you never bothered to tell me that Arianna Smith was your married name? Doesn't that strike you as funny?"

After a quick swipe at her eyes, Arianna addressed her husband. Ex-husband. "Carter, we had our chance. It didn't work. We blew it a thousand times, and you know it. We've been through all this—"

Old Carter seemed to hit his limit, if the spectacular purple color of his face was any indication. "Who is this guy, Arianna?" he roared.

"It's none of your business anymore!"

"Are you in love with him?"

"Yes." She said it simply and quietly, with no shame and even less ambivalence. "I'm in love with him, and it's past time for us both to move on."

The dude's face crumpled and quickly reformed, all except a muscle in his jaw, which flexed convulsively. Joshua watched the scene, strangely unmoved. A man and his ex-wife, the woman he still loved. Nothing new at all; so banal it was practically a yawn-fest. What else wasn't new? The betrayal in Joshua's life. *Guess what, Joshua? Someone else in your life isn't who he or she seems to be. Oh, really? Yawn.*

It was all the same; it would never change. He'd been a fool to think it would.

"That's how it is, then?" Carter asked Arianna.

"Yes," she told him. "That's how it is. I'm sorry."

Carter snorted. "Yeah. So am I." Dropping his head, he stared at the floor for a minute, maybe to give this whole mess a minute to settle. He rubbed his hand over his scalp once or twice and then looked up, his eyes such a hard glitter that they might have been diamonds frozen in ice cubes lodged inside the heart of a North Atlantic glacier. "Well, Joshua or Dawson or whatever the hell your name is…she's all yours. I hope that works out better for you than it did for me."

Joshua wanted to knock the fool's teeth in, but he'd spent too much time trying to get out of prison to do something stupid enough to send him back in.

Carter started to go, but Arianna, in another of her presto-chango surprises for the day, reached out to stop him with her hand on his arm. He froze, rigid as one of Michelangelo's statues, and the snarling beast inside Joshua wanted to rip that arm out of its socket as a punishment for receiving one of Arianna's touches.

"Carter," she said, all beseeching urgency, as though she couldn't live one more goddamn minute without making up with her ex-husband. "I don't want to leave it like this. Please. We loved each other once, didn't we?"

Carter wavered.

Joshua watched the touching little scene, bitterly wishing he could kick his own ass for stupidity. Arianna claimed she loved Joshua now, but she'd loved this other guy once, enough to marry him. So much for forever, eh? And here was her ex-husband, the man who'd once been the center of her existence, and Joshua hadn't even known the guy existed until five minutes ago.

Staring at the two of them together, Joshua imagined it all: a wedding, the blushing bride, the looks between them, the kisses and the touches. Bile rose in his throat, thick enough to choke him to death.

Married. Arianna had been married. To someone else. And he'd stupidly thought that he was the only man she'd ever loved.

Can you say *chump?*

Carter, meanwhile, softened like a taffy chew under the hopeful earnestness in Arianna's face. The punk. Joshua watched, disbelieving, as Arianna eased into the guy's arms and then—

Ain't that some shit?

They hugged, one of those lengthy, end-of-the-world embraces that said everything while saying nothing. It went on long enough for Joshua to die several excruciating deaths, and then suddenly it was over, and Carter the Noble was letting Arianna go, something Joshua knew he himself would never be man enough to do, no matter the circumstances.

"Take care of yourself," Carter told her.

"You, too," she said.

Joshua wanted to curse them both to hell for eternity, but all that came out of his mouth was an incoherent sound of disgust.

Carter peeled his riveted gaze away from Arianna,

flashed Joshua a final killing glare and strode out. Arianna watched him go and then turned slowly to Joshua, taking forever to meet his eyes.

There was nothing to say, nothing that could possibly be said. So he let his eyes do the talking and didn't try to hide any of it: the sharp and bewildering sense of betrayal, the mistrust, the bleeding pain.

Let this be a lesson to him: no one was ever what he or she seemed.

Sensing the way the wind was blowing, she hurried forward, tears sparkling again, and tried to put her hand on his arm—that same hand that had just been on another man's arm.

Joshua stepped back, and then he wheeled around and retraced Carter's steps, out of the room and away from her.

"You've been drinking," Arianna said.

After giving Joshua a wide berth for several hours, avoiding him during dinner and waiting until the rest of the household went to bed, she'd tracked him here to the study, a room she usually avoided. Like the library, it was full of books. Unlike the library, it was heavy with oppressive wood molding and furniture, leather chairs and sofas and, yes, the obligatory stuffed animal heads—water buffalo, zebra and lioness—on the walls. Old Reynolds Warner had probably meant this room to be a bastion of masculinity back in the day, but the ambience was of unrelenting gloom, especially now.

Although it was dark outside, it seemed darker in here somehow, and the dim light of a single lamp in the corner intensified the effect. It threw harsh shadows onto Joshua's face as he sat in a wingback chair, making him appear more dangerous, which was saying a lot. His eyes were moody, his face grim. A snifter of brandy was gripped loosely in his hand, and he had his arm draped over the arm of the chair.

Staring at her where she hovered in the doorway, he raised his glass and drank. Deeply. She could almost feel the burn in her own throat and the rush to her head. Virtual brandy wouldn't be enough to get her through this conversation, though, and she wished she had a real one. About ten ounces should do it.

The drink cart sat right next to Joshua, heavy with a glittering array of crystal decanters and bottles. If she had a little more courage, she'd march over there and pour herself a stiff one, but doing that would put her too close to him, and the look in his eyes was lethal enough from here, thanks.

The wounded bear was in full effect tonight, and she'd waltzed right into his cave with a steak strapped to her chest. Maybe a smarter woman would've left him alone to lick his injuries for a little while longer, but of course if she'd been smart she'd've told him about Carter the night they met instead of letting the information swell to *Titanic*-sized proportions.

His glass drained, Joshua leaned over to the cart for a refill, his lips stretching in a crooked smile devoid of humor. "Well, you see, Mrs. Smith—"

"Don't call me that."

"—I needed a drink tonight. Know why?"

"Joshua—"

"It's because the one person in the world I thought would never betray me, the woman I—"

He caught himself, his words screeching to a halt.

Oh, God. The need to hear that sentence from his lips ate her up inside, as though she'd swallowed a school of piranha and their cruel little teeth were slicing away at her guts. "Say it, Joshua. The woman you what? Love?"

That terrible smile widened until the ugliness of it threatened to consume his face. "First of all, I don't believe in love, Mrs. Smith—"

"Bull."

"—and second, falling in love with a woman who just got divorced ten minutes ago is pretty stupid, don't you think?"

This was all bravado. She knew it, but that didn't help any more than an aspirin would help with a broken femur. "You're mad." She paused but, hell, she'd come this far—why punk out now? "And hurt. I'm sorry."

He raised his glass in an ironic and insulting toast. "You don't have the power to hurt me, beautiful little lying Arianna. No one does."

Okay. That did it.

Stalking into the room at last, she slammed the door behind her—no need for the whole household to hear this—and crossed over to him in three long strides. That glass was one inch from his lips when she snatched it away and, without pausing to think, hurled it at that freaking ugly lion's head on the wall, which she hated as much as she currently hated Joshua. *Bingo.* It shattered in a spectacular shower of flying glass and brandy that made her feel much better.

"Bullshit," she told him calmly. "Everything you just said is bullshit."

He went utterly still, explosively quiet. For two or three long seconds, that hostile gaze pounded her the way the waves at the Cape of Good Hope pound hapless ships. When he spoke again, his low, accusatory voice crawled up her spine, making her want to squirm.

"You know what I think is bullshit? Screwing me

and not mentioning—not even *once*—that you had a husband."

"I don't have a husband."

"You see?" That crooked smile again. "Bullshit."

Taking all the time in the world, he reached for a fresh glass, and that was more than she could take. She started to snatch this one, too, but he was too quick for her this time and their hands scrabbled together, locked on the glass. With a final wrench, he tore it out of her grip and clamped down on her wrist with his free hand.

"You're trying my patience, princess."

The maneuvering had culminated with her leaning over him in the chair, their faces a breathless inch apart. Her wrist might have been on the receiving end of his anger, but he wanted her, too. Maybe more than he hated her right now, he wanted her. It was in the tension thrumming through his muscles and the hard glitter in his eyes, and that want shivered through her, forcing her own body to respond with heat.

She reined herself in, hard. They'd spent too much time having sex when they should have been talking. That was about to change.

"I got married my junior year in college—"

All that vibrating passion and rage made his body jerk, but she refused to let that scare her into backing down.

"—and I didn't know what I was doing or who I was. I thought I was in love—"

"The way you currently think you're in love with me? Like that?"

"—but really I gave more thought to the wedding dress than I did to the man or the marriage. We tried to make it work, but we're too different, and he talked a good game but never followed through on his promises and never let me become part of his life. We should never've gotten married in the first place."

"Oh," he said with exaggerated understanding. "So it was a starter marriage."

She winced. He had a real talent for putting the worst possible spin on things. "I never viewed my marriage as temporary or disposable—"

"Well, that's not strictly true, is it, seeing how you're divorced?"

"—but I'm not going to spend the rest of my life with the wrong man because I made a mistake when I was twenty-one."

"How fascinating." He twiddled his fingers on the arm of his chair with obvious impatience. "Tell me, just out of curiosity, what does your loving ex-husband do? Obviously you met at Stanford, right, but what does he do now?"

And the hits just kept on coming. Man, she hated to tell him, knowing what he'd do with the information. "He graduated from Yale Med. He's a surgical resident."

Aaannnd there it was: the hardening of Joshua's features, the palpable crashing of his ego. It was amazing how well she could read him. Truly a gift.

"Right." That horrible crooked smile stretched his lips again. "He probably doesn't have a prison record or a tattoo on his neck, does he?"

"What can I do?" she asked helplessly, sinking to her knees in front of him and holding the unforgiving hardness of his thighs. It was a dangerous move, she knew; he could snarl and lash out and she could draw back two stumps where her arms used to be. But fearsome as he was, she couldn't resist reaching out after they'd come so far together. She wasn't going to lose him now. "I don't want him. You know how I feel about you."

"That's the thing, sweet Arianna." Underneath all that

anger, something in his expression softened, just a hair. Cupping her face, he stroked her cheek with his thumb. Gently at first, and then harder, stretching her flesh so that her lips peeled back from her teeth. She didn't even care—she was that desperate. "That's the thing. I don't know anything. I've never known anything. I've never gotten it right. I knew Bishop was my father, but he wasn't. I knew Reynolds Warner was just my father's boss, but he wasn't. I knew Andrew was just my friend, but he wasn't." Here his fingers tightened even further, digging into her face. "I knew you were sweet and honest, but you weren't."

Her heart turned over, dropping like a stone through a layer of tissue paper.

"I knew you could be everything to me." He ran his thumb over her bottom lip with such unspeakable tenderness that her longing tightened and coiled, settling finally in the clenching inner muscles between her thighs. But then a light switched off behind his eyes, sending an Arctic wind through the room. "But you can't."

Shoving her face away, he let her go and surged to his feet.

No. They wouldn't throw this away. "Joshua—"

"Why didn't you tell me?" he roared, wheeling back around. "Do you think it's okay to blindside me the way everyone else in my life always has? Do you think I can trust you now? *Why didn't you tell me?*"

A sapling had a better chance of bearing up under a level 5 tornado than she did before Joshua's rage, but she had to try. "I didn't want to tell you the first night—"

"Yeah? And what about every goddamned night since then?"

"There was so much going on, with Bishop's emergency—"

"That was weeks ago, precious. You'll have to do better than that."

"I know it sounds lame," she said, her rising frustration and desperation making her flounder. How could she explain the most stupid thing she'd ever done in her life, outside of getting married so young? "I'm not proud of it. But the longer I didn't tell you, the bigger the secret got. And I knew you had problems with secrets—"

"How insightful. Guess that Yale education paid off for you, eh?"

"—and I didn't expect to fall this hard for you so fast—"

"Do you get how ridiculous this sounds?"

How could she deny it? "Yes."

"You know the weird thing, Arianna? I was getting funny thoughts up here—" he jabbed two fingers against his temple "—and I can't believe I'm even saying this, but here it is: I was thinking about marrying you."

"Oh, God," she breathed.

"But I thought I'd be your *first* husband. Not your *current* husband."

All her pride did a spectacular swan dive out the window. Throwing herself at him, she wrapped her arms around his neck and pulled him down so she could kiss his throbbing jaw.

"Please forgive me," she whispered between kisses. "I'll do anything."

To her agonized astonishment, he grabbed her up the way a drowning man would latch on to a buoy. One burst of movement had her in his arms and nearly bent double with the force of his passion. He rained biting kisses all over her face and into her mouth, and his chest vibrated with animalistic growls.

Joyous relief swelled out of her on a laugh, and she held

him closer, digging her fingers into that cottony nest of hair at his nape.

His hands went to her butt, pressing her up against a rigid erection and rubbing her sweet spot there, just *there,* until sharp sparks of pleasure fanned out from her sex. Unsatisfied, he gathered up the back of her dress, baring her to the waist, and slid his hands underneath her panties, palming her, hard. Those sparks intensified and she cried out, teetering on a razor's edge.

"I'm always happy to screw you whenever you want, Ari." His warm palms kneaded her again. "That doesn't mean I forgive you."

All her hopes and passion went up in an incinerating burst of light. Could love swing around to hate this quickly? Because, just that quick, she despised him.

She smacked her hands against his chest in a silent demand. When he let her go, she smoothed her dress and embraced the cool anger that was so much better than tears. Taking a minute, just to see, just to be sure, she looked into his eyes and was gratified to discover that, under the thick layer of his bravado, his wounds were throbbing and inflamed. Bleeding. The poor man hadn't yet discovered that he couldn't hurt her without hurting himself worse.

"You know, Dawson," she began.

"Back to Dawson now, are we?"

"Yeah." She ignored that sardonic raised brow and concentrated instead on the telltale harshness of his breath and the color in his cheeks. "This dark, unforgiving, vengeful side of you is Dawson all the way. And the thing is, *Dawson,* this isn't about my mistake in not telling you."

"Really?" That damned brow of his inched higher.

"It's about you licking your wounds, again. It's about you being your favorite thing—a victim."

A warning rumble radiated out from his chest.

"It's about you being the perfect one and the only one who's ever allowed to make mistakes. It's about you being the judge and jury for everyone else."

His fists clenched. In his face, meanwhile, both brows had dropped to a single menacing black slash above his eyes, and his lips had all but disappeared.

"It's about you being all talk and no action despite your yammering about new beginnings. Which is sad, really. Because we've got something here, and I know that you're the best thing that's ever happened to me—"

He blinked.

"—but you're too bitter—or maybe stupid—to admit that I'm the best thing that's ever happened to you."

They stared at each other. She felt his anguish, but since her heart was currently a pile of rubble, she didn't much care at the moment. After a few seconds, the tears burning in her throat demanded to make an appearance. Since she'd be tarred and feathered in the nearest town square before she cried in front of him, it was probably a good time to go.

"If you ever decide to get rid of Dawson once and for all," she told him as she walked out, "you let me know."

Chapter 14

Joshua banged into the kitchen two mornings later, still mad at the world and hung over from a second night of drinking, which was funny considering how, during his party years, he'd been able to drink his way through a six-pack and a fifth of Jack without blinking an eye. Seeing Bishop and Arnetta already there, sitting at the banquette, didn't help his mood, especially when they caught sight of him and their delighted little grins evaporated. Bishop, he realized, had just successfully spooned another bite of grits into his mouth and was now chewing. That was probably what all the happy-happy was about, and he shouldn't ruin it by being a punk.

"Hey." He tried to smile because he was thrilled with this progress even if his own personal life was in the toilet. "Great job, Pop."

"Your father will be eating us out of house and home

if he keeps up like this," Arnetta announced, beaming. "This is his third bowl."

"Yeah?" Joshua grabbed a coffee mug; a nice shot of caffeine would help flush some of last night's alcohol out of his system, right? "That's good news."

Bishop swallowed, frowned and, with painstaking care, raised his napkin to wipe his mouth. "What's wrong, Josh-a?"

"Nothing." Filling his cup, Joshua took a scalding sip and cursed. "I'm great."

"You lie." Bishop's wizened eyes narrowed. "Ari pr-problem?"

Arnetta, who'd been sipping from a cup of tea, clanked it back down, looked between the two men and spluttered, "Arianna? What's Arianna got to do with—" Joshua's misery plus his burning face were apparently dead giveaways, because her eyes widened with sudden understanding. "Oh, my heavens. You and Arianna? Oh, my."

Bishop ignored this distraction and focused all his attention on Joshua. "Tell me, son."

The use of the *S* word grated on Joshua's nerves because, seriously, did the old guy think he was his shrink now? They'd been getting along pretty well, yeah, and trying again and all that, but he was a grown man who didn't need to explain this latest stunning betrayal and corresponding hurt to anybody.

"I need a little space." Abandoning the coffee idea, he decided to just leave before things got worse. *"Pop."*

Bishop didn't have the sense to leave well enough alone. Maybe that had been a casualty of the stroke. Whatever it was, he plowed right ahead, calling after Joshua as he headed for the door. "I help you."

That was it.

Joshua wheeled back around and headed for the banquette, banging the wall with his fist as he went. Then he planted his hands on the table and leaned down in Bishop's face.

"Great. You want to help?" Yeah, he was doing a spectacular swan dive off the deep end here, but he felt like he'd earned the right. "Well maybe, *Dad,* you can tell me why no one in my life has ever been who he or she was supposed to be. You got an answer for that? Can you explain why I'm surrounded by people with secrets and hidden agendas? Huh? Or maybe you can help by telling me who I can trust and who I can't trust. How about that?"

Bishop didn't blink an eye before all this unvarnished fury. "Ari hurt you."

"Ari's *married,*" Joshua roared.

"Divorced."

Arnetta's calm clarification only made him more manic. "*Divorced.* Thanks so much. Maybe you can tell me why everyone knew that but me. Anyone have an answer for that? Anyone?"

Bishop smiled with such infinite understanding and wisdom that Joshua almost couldn't bear to meet his gaze. "You ask questions wrong." Bishop scrunched up his face and rearranged his words. "You ask wrong questions. Ari did her best. I did my best. We messed up. Question is, why can't *you*—" he pointed a gnarled index finger at Joshua's nose "—forgive people for mistakes?"

With that, a lightning bolt of sudden clarity—about five million volts' worth—struck Joshua on the head, nearly knocking him out. He was still reeling when Bishop stood, grabbed Joshua's face in his hand, planted a kiss on his cheek and left the kitchen with Arnetta.

* * *

Another Saturday night at Heather Hill, another charity shindig.

Oh, joy.

This was a small gala, if a gala could be small. It was either for cancer research or the local arts association—Arianna couldn't remember which, and if she could remember, she wouldn't care.

Charity…giving…rah, rah, rah. Big freaking deal.

After putting in an appearance in her sexy little black dress—not that there was any real point to looking nice or, hell, basic grooming these days—she'd eyed the desserts (no appetite), declined a glass of champagne (not thirsty) and decamped out here, to the terrace nearest the greenhouse.

Not to brood, or anything. She wasn't *brooding.* That was *his* game. Joshua/Dawson/Whoever. In the last several days she'd simplified matters and just referred to him as the Jerk when she thought of him, which was either all the time or once per second, whichever was more frequent.

But it was hard not to…remember. That's what she was doing. Remembering. This night was balmy and starlit, and so was that one. The same jazz combo had played both parties, and don't get her started on pasta bars. Resting her elbows on the stone ledge, she tightened her filmy wrap and glared off in the distance. Stupid party. Why did she have to be subjected to this nonsense when she was miserable and would prefer hiding in the cottage with the sheet over her head? And why—

Heavy male footsteps came up behind her, making her jump like an Olympic sprinter out of the starting block. When her feet hit the ground again, she spun and discovered him standing there. Joshua. Because it was impossible to think of him as the Jerk when he wore a great black tuxedo, had a spark of a smile in his dark eyes and held two bowls of something chocolatey in his hands.

"Weren't you going to say hi to me?" he asked.

Oh, God. Oh, holy God. Mother of—

"No," she managed, her jaw still hovering around her navel. "I wasn't."

"Hmm." He handed her one of the bowls, which she took because some weird sort of autopilot had taken over her body and was now firmly in charge. "Well, it's a good thing I followed you out here, isn't it?"

She couldn't speak.

"Here." Reaching for her waist, he swung her up onto the wall. He also, fortunately, prevented her from toppling backward and falling to her death when her jellified spine gave way and refused to hold her upright.

When the dust settled, he'd created a space for himself between her legs and kept his hands somewhat lower on her body, more butt than waist. Watching her with that intent gaze, he put his bowl on the ledge and did the same with hers. From there it was simple enough for him to step closer and pull her into his arms and for her to wrap her thighs around his.

She stared at him, trying to sound coherent when joyous sobs threatened to erupt from her throat. "What should I call you tonight?" she questioned. "I've been thinking of you as the Jerk, but you probably don't care for that."

A smile broke across his face, the most beautiful sight the universe could produce. There was no angst in that smile, no bitterness or anger, nothing but smile.

"How about you call me Joshua? It's my name. Well… it will be again soon. I filed the paperwork."

"Interesting."

That smile faded, leaving only absolute focus on his face. "Glad you think so."

"I've had a name change, too. I'm going back to Davies. My maiden name."

"Interesting."

"So, *Joshua,*" she said, tilting her hips just enough to bring her sweet spot up against the deliciously hard bulge of his groin and enjoying the corresponding hitch in his breath, "is this you forgiving me?"

Those hips circled and thrust, making her cry out. He dipped his head, speaking against her lips. "This is me asking you to forgive me."

"For what?" It was important to make wrongdoers recite their crimes, right? Plus she didn't want to make this whole exercise too easy for him.

"Being unforgiving."

A tiny laugh bubbled up to her lips, but her swelling heart wouldn't allow much more than that. "You were pretty unforgiving."

"I know. I'm sorry."

"I'm sorry, too. For not telling you."

"You're forgiven."

"Thank God."

"Yeah." He leaned his forehead against hers. "Thank you, God. Thank you."

The raspy emotion in his voice was so heartfelt it just killed her. With a crazy half-laugh, half-sob combination, she pulled his head down, and he nuzzled his face into the curve of her neck. His glasses were hard and uncomfortable, but she didn't even care.

This was heaven, and she hadn't had to die to get there.

Some time passed while he held her. She lost herself in his scent and the hard embrace of his body, and oh,

God, there was nothing like it. Never had been and never could be.

"I knew," she said in his ear. "The first night I saw you, I knew…" She trailed off, helpless to find words for this and afraid she'd sound silly if she did.

"Knew what, baby?"

He drew back so he could see her, forcing more intimacy, and she discovered that when this big teddy bear looked at her with all that warmth and adoration, even if he'd never said he loved her, things weren't so scary after all.

"I knew you were the one for me," she said simply, shrugging. "The only one."

A shudder rippled through him as he looked to the skies and the stars overhead. "Thank you," he said again, and then he was kissing her.

It was an onslaught, something she could never have braced for. His mouth, hot and skilled, took hers in every way imaginable, sucking, biting and licking her top lip, then her bottom, then both lips together and then, finally, planting his hand in her hair, angling her head and delving deep into her, as though he was determined to reach every part of her body through just her mouth.

Only when all the breath had left her lungs and she'd begun rubbing her aching breasts against his chest and scraping his nails across his scalp did he pull back enough to speak.

"I was wondering," he rasped, "if maybe we could go to the greenhouse."

"Yeah. We could do that."

Same drill as before. She clamped her legs tight around his hips and he swung her around and hurried through the door with her, into their private inner sanctum.

She didn't let him go. Not until he'd navigated through

the dark and over to the bench, their bench, and laid her gently on it, flat on her back. Wasting no time, he shrugged out of his jacket, chucked it to the ground, sat at her hip and ran his hands over her body in an endless massage that made her writhe with pleasure.

Resting her arms up by her head so she could arch for him, she moaned, not caring how loud she got or how much she gave of herself. He could have it all. He'd always owned it all anyway.

"I love you," she said when he ran his hands over her breasts, squeezing them together and then pushing them apart, biting her nipples through the thin silk of her dress and the thinner silk of her bra. "God, I love you so much. You have no idea."

He laughed or growled—she couldn't tell which. The only thing she knew for sure was that the sound was joyous, triumphant, and if she could get him to make that wonderful noise merely by telling him how she felt, she'd be happy to do it again.

"I love you," she said when his hands gripped her hips and he buried his face in her belly, biting her there, too.

But her voice could only hold out for so long, especially when he went to work on her panties, sliding them down her legs and off. "I love—" she began again, but when he kissed her there, spreading her thighs and loving her sex the way he'd loved her mouth, her thoughts spiraled out of control and sentences were impossible.

Her cries grew louder; she couldn't help it. Her body's tension knotted and coiled, pooling in that one perfect spot down low, but even the growing ecstasy wouldn't shut her up, not now.

Did he understand? Did he know? Was it enough yet?

"Love," she murmured, pulling his hair so he'd come

closer and stop torturing her beyond her endurance. "Ah, God, Joshua…love you. I love—"

He slid his way back up her body, rubbing and touching her everywhere, owning her so that it wasn't even her body anymore—it was his. And then there was the rough, urgent slide of his zipper, and he levered over her, resting on his elbows. Pausing long enough to look at her with gleaming, unsmiling eyes, he kissed her again, slow and easy.

The hot glide of his tongue into her mouth was all it took. Her inner muscles clenched in tiny spasms that grew into such piercing pleasure that her womb contracted and her body convulsed.

He held her, keeping her close as she rode it out. But when her limp body stilled and she caught her breath, the litany started again because she could never say it enough and he needed to know. It didn't matter if he never said it to her—she saw his love when he looked at her the way he'd been doing—as long as he trusted how she felt.

"I love you," she said again. "So much…so mu—"

"I love you, too."

"—much… So much…so—*what?*"

Another licking kiss, during which she though she felt his mouth smile against hers. "You heard me."

As nice as his tongue deep in her mouth was, they needed to get this straight. Pulling back as much as she could with the hard bench at her back, she stared up at him, pushed her hair out of her face and tried not to be too needy.

"Say it again," she demanded.

This was no time for joking, and he knew it. The emotion, in fact, seemed to overcome him, and his nostrils flared. She watched, fascinated, as he took a minute to bite his trembling lower lip and get himself together. And then the strongest man she knew, this teddy bear, blinked back his tears and stared her in the face.

She saw it all, even before he said it.

"I. Love. You."

And she didn't want to ruin the moment with anything negative like, say, sobbing or doubts, but she did both. Happy sobs, but still sobs. "But you don't believe in love. You said—"

He laughed. "You're rubbing my face in it now? Is that what's going on here?"

"No, but—"

"Arianna. You know I love you. You know I've always loved you. Don't you?"

"Yes?" she said, and sobbed again.

For reasons incomprehensible to her, he thought this was funny, too, and was still laughing up until he took the broad head of his penis and stroked it against her thick folds, which were over-sensitized and tingly. Like magic, all the breath whooshed out of both of them, and they gasped.

"God," she said as he eased his way inside her body, one slow inch at a time.

"Yeah." His voice was hoarse now, barely more than a whisper. *"God."*

His hips surged and eased, surged and eased, and the pleasure began to build again, hotter this time, brighter. Brushing his pants and underwear down his legs a little and out of her way, she clamped her hands on his bare ass as it flexed. And then she drew up her legs, pulled him closer and forced him deeper.

"Don't stop," she said. "Don't ever stop."

"That reminds me." He broke his rhythm while he spoke, and the effort of holding himself back showed in the sheen of sweat across his forehead. "I promised myself I'd spend every night with you, if possible. Forever. That would probably involve, you know, something like marriage. At some point. When you're ready."

"You want to marry me?"

"Yeah. I want to marry you."

"Good."

They smiled at each other for one delicious moment, and then she nudged her hips against his to remind him where he'd left off, and they flowed together in the perfect rhythm.

* * * * *